TANGLED IN

CHARLOTTE'S WEB

(A SHORT STORY SEXCAPADE)

by

Tina Mitchell

Printed in the United States of America

Cover Design by Cassy Roop @ Pink Ink Designs

Copy Editing, Proofreading, & Interior Formatting by Jessica Filippi (www.jessicafilippi.com)

Email: itsteetymethewriter@gmail.com

Website & Blog: itsteetymethewriter.wordpress.com

ISBN: 9781794676077
Imprint: Independently published

ii

CONTENTS

CHAPTER ONE

It all started one October; the fall leaves had Diane mesmerized. She was staring out the window in deep thought, reminiscing about the day Roger and she had met.

She remembered pulling up to the gas station, and when she looked over she saw this white guy bopping his head, listening to some rap music. It was loud. She remembered thinking, *This wannabe thug*. She got out of her car, went in, and paid. Back at the pump, her gas cap was on so tight she couldn't get it off. She was struggling and struggling, but she refused to ask the guy with the loud music for help. By the time she looked up, he was already behind her, reaching for the gas cap. He turned it and it came off easily. He smelled so good. He was also tall, handsome, and sexy and his body felt good close to hers. She thought, *What is this white boy doing in the hood?* and then her next thought was, *He has swag*.

She smiled and thanked him for his help.

"No problem, what's your name, beautiful?" he said.

"Diane, and yours?"

"Roger."

She extended her hand to shake his. "Thank you again, Roger."

"My pleasure."

She thought that was the end of it, but as she walked toward her car, he called out to her. "Hey Diane, can I call you and take you out sometime?"

"Hmm," she considered. "I'm not sure I want to give you my number. I'm very busy."

"Oh, it's like that," he said, and they both laughed. "I'm very busy myself. But maybe we can make some time for one another. I'm not taking no for an answer."

"Well, since you're not taking no for an answer, give me your number and I'll call you."

He reached out and took her phone, entering his number into her contacts. "Ok, that's cool. I'm going to expect a call soon. Have a nice day, gorgeous."

She smiled and blushed. "Thank you—you too!"

Diane's memories were interrupted by something outside the window, a man slowly driving by and looking at the houses. She stepped back behind the curtain just to be nosy. First, she had never seen that car before in the neighborhood, and second, if anything went down, she could give the police a description of the car.

The guy's car crawled slowly up the street until it reached Mr. and Mrs. Web's house. Diane had spoken to Lloyd last week, and she knew he was going out of town, but she didn't recall him mentioning anything about anyone coming, so she wondered who this could be.

The guy got out his car and started looking around. He was a well-dressed man, clean cut—young and handsome, she might add—but she thought it rather odd that he was going around the back of the house. She guessed that he could be selling something or doing a consultation for some yard work. She thought nothing further of it and went to take a hot bath. After her bath and a nap, she looked again and the car was gone.

*****

It was 5:00 pm and Roger was on his way home from work. Diane had just finished cooking dinner ten minutes earlier when he walked in the door.

"Di—I'm home."

"Hey, I'm in the kitchen, go wash up for dinner!"

A few moments later, Roger walked back into the kitchen and gave her a kiss.

"How was your day?" she asked.

"Long. How was your day?"

"Mine was interesting, but the most interesting part was that Charlotte had company today. I don't recall Lloyd mentioning doing anything to the house."

"Diane, I'm sure she doesn't tell you everything. Mind your own business. You don't know what's going on and please don't speculate."

"I know, I know, you're right. Let's eat."

"Yes, please, it was a long day."

After dinner Diane cleaned the kitchen, and then checked the doors and windows. She glanced out to the street and noticed the same car again. She didn't say anything about it, just pulled the blinds closed, because her husband had told her to mind her own business. She went upstairs and saw that Roger was asleep, so she put her night gown on, pulled her hair in a ponytail, and went to bed.

*****

The next morning Roger was gone early. Diane got up and did her normal routine.

Lately, she'd had writer's block and couldn't seem to get any inspiration. So she decided to go to the grocery store to get a few things for dinner, and guess who she ran into? Charlotte.

Diane saw her down at the other end of the aisle, her long, bleach blonde hair hanging almost to her flat ass. Diane walked up behind her. "Hey, Charlotte, how are you?"

It must have surprised her, since she jumped a little before turning around. "Hey, girly," she said, giving Diane a quick hug. "I'm fine, and you?"

Diane noticed Charlotte had gotten more work done on her fake tits and some work done on her face, her smile looked stiff.

"I'm great. How's things been going with you and Lloyd?"

"It is what it is. He's fine, doing what he does best: work."

"Well, you know you can't change that."

"I guess you're right. How's your workaholic husband?"

Diane laughed. "He's great, doing what he does best: work!"

"Well, it was good seeing you, girl," she said, aiming her cart toward the registers. "I have to get going. You and Roger have to come over for dinner soon!"

"Ok, that sounds great," Diane said. "See you soon."

As Charlotte walked away her phone rang. She seemed to be in a rush—to go where, Diane didn't know, since she doesn't work. Whoever she was talking to on the phone, she was whispering. Diane could hardly hear her but she could tell it wasn't Lloyd. But then she remembered what her husband said again: mind her own business. All she knew was that something was up with Charlotte, and she couldn't put her finger on it.

*****

Later that day, Roger called to let Diane know he would be late and to not wait up for him. It wasn't the first time—and she knew it wouldn't be the last—that he had to work late. It hadn't bothered her when she was traveling, doing her book signings and radio and TV interviews, but now that she hadn't written a book in a year things had changed between them.

Roger and Diane didn't have any children. Diane was very young when she had to have a partial hysterectomy; it was so painful to hear that they may not be able to have a baby. They wanted one so badly. Although the doctors said that they had a 50/50 chance of conceiving, it hadn't happened in five years of trying. Roger said that having children doesn't matter, but sometimes when they saw other families and friends with children, he got this look in his eyes that told Diane different. To add fuel to the fire, Diane wrote bestselling children books.

They had done well for themselves. Roger and Diane had been together for fifteen years, married for twelve. It had been up and down; they had their good days and their bad days. One thing she was certain about is he loved her—and that's all that mattered.

Diane's phone rang, startling her out of her thoughts. It was Charlotte, saying that Lloyd would be returning that night from his trip and he wanted to invite her and Roger over for dinner.

"Great, we would love to"

"I want to ask a favor," she added. "If he asks if we ran into each other at the grocery store and we returned home at the same time, could you say yes?"

"Yes, sure—is everything ok?"

"Yes. Lloyd's just getting older and he's becoming very insecure. I try to tell him he has nothing to worry about but I'm sure coming from you it will make him feel more at ease. Will you two be over for dinner?"

"Yes, we will. What time?"

"7:00 pm."

"Ok, see you then."

As soon as Diane hung up with Charlotte, she called Roger.

"Hi, gorgeous."

"Hi honey, I wanted to let you know to come straight home tonight. Lloyd is coming home today and Charlotte wants us to come to dinner at 7:00 pm."

"Ok, I will be home by 6:00. See ya."

Diane didn't say anything about it to Roger, but she couldn't stop thinking about the favor Charlotte had asked of her and the comment she made that Lloyd would be more at ease if it came from her. *Why would that be the case?* she thought. *Since we're both black?*

Anyway, the truth was that Diane had seen Charlotte early in the day at the grocery store, and she wasn't home when Diane got home. Her car was gone for several hours. *Why did she want me to lie to Lloyd about it? What was she hiding?* Diane thought. Minding her own business was getting harder and harder.

*****

When Roger walked in at 6:00, Diane was dressed and ready to go. He went upstairs to change, and then they headed across the street to the Web's house.

Lloyd greeted them at the door with his bright smile and his sexy bald head. Lloyd stood six foot one with broad shoulders and fit frame, toppling over Diane as he leaned over and kissed her on the cheek and extended his hand to shake Roger's. "Hey, guys!"

"Hello," Diane said. "You're back! It's good to see you."

"Hey man, how you been?" Roger said, handing Lloyd the bottle of wine they brought. Although Lloyd was smiling, Roger noticed the stress on Lloyd's face. He has known Lloyd a long time and something was bothering him.

"Come in. Charlotte! Our favorite neighbors are here!"

Charlotte came in from the kitchen wiping her hands. She leaned in to kiss first Diane, then Roger, on the cheek. Diane followed her to the kitchen while Lloyd and Roger went out back.

Lloyd handed Roger a shot of whiskey from the wet bar they had set up on the patio. "So, Roger, how are things going at Roger's DJ's?"

"Things are great; we were just featured in Time Out magazine and business has been booming."

"Congratulations, man, you worked hard."

"Thank you, thank you. How are things going with you at the firm?"

Lloyd sighed. "Things are going. We lost a big contract, and I've been working extra hard night and day to get them to reconsider. If we don't it could hurt us tremendously."

"Well, let me know if there's anything I can do to help."

"Thanks, man, I appreciate it. Come on, let's go see if dinner's ready."

*****

In the kitchen, Charlotte and Diane were sharing a glass of wine while she put the finishing touches on dinner. At the sound of the back door closing, she said, "I hear the guys coming—oh, and Diane, don't forget when Lloyd asks about yesterday, let him know you saw me."

"Don't worry, I won't forget." Diane laughed, somewhat nervously, and Charlotte laughed too.

Charlotte refilled my wineglass. "Thank you, this is much needed," Diane commented.

"Yes indeed," she said, with another laugh. "Let's sit down."

*****

"That was delicious, Charlotte," Roger said, as he placed his fork and knife on the empty plate.

"Yes," Diane agreed, "that beef brisket was wonderful."

Charlotte smiled over the rim of her wineglass. "Thank you; its Lloyd's favorite. "Is everyone ready for dessert? We're having strawberry crème brulèe—another one of Lloyd's favorites."

"Yes, it is," Lloyd said, rubbing his hands together and smiling.

"Anything for you, darling," Charlotte responded, touching Lloyd's hand.

As they were finishing up dessert, Lloyd turned to Diane. "Diane, I guess Charlotte picked all this up today at the grocery store when you two saw each other."

"Yes," she said, "it was a surprise running into her there."

Charlotte made eye contact and smiled at Diane.

"Great," Lloyd said, his face relaxing into a smile. He slid his chair out to get up and start collecting the dishes.

Charlotte stood up quickly. "No, the ladies have this. You guys relax, and we'll take care of this."

"Thanks," he said as he kissed Charlotte on the cheek.

As he and Roger sat back down outside, Lloyd asked, "Roger, have you seen anything unusual around my house?"

"No man, why?"

"Things have been a little off with me and Charlotte, and now she's complaining that I work too much. I don't understand—if I don't work, we won't be able to maintain her lifestyle. Charlotte spends a lot of money."

"Man, don't worry," Roger said, touching Lloyd shoulder. "Everything is OK, we all go through stuff." He looked at his watch, "Man, it's getting late and I have an early meeting in the morning. We should get going."

"Ok man," Lloyd said, "thanks for joining us for dinner."

Roger and Lloyd go back in the house and find the ladies in the living room.

"Ok, ladies, time to break things up," Roger said.

"Oh no, you guys have to go so soon?" said Charlotte.

"Yes, I have early meetings in the morning," he replied.

"Charlotte, dinner was great. Thank you, Lloyd, it was good seeing you," Diane said as they walked to the foyer.

"Ok, see you soon!" Charlotte said before closing the door behind them. "Oh! Lloyd honey, I forgot to ask them about—"

She started to turn away from the door, startled that Lloyd was right behind her. Before she could finish her sentence, Lloyd grabbed her around her neck and started choking her.

"Lloyd, you're hurting me! Stop!"

"Shut up!" He put his mouth close to her ear, and in a low, seething voice told her, "If I find out you've been lying to me, I will kill you—you understand?"

"You're hurting me," she said, tears rolling down her face. "I can't breathe."

"You keep it up, and I will take your last breath!" He threw her to the floor and stormed off to his study.

Charlotte went upstairs to take a shower. She leaned against the cold tiles, crying and thinking about what had come over Lloyd in the past few years. He'd been very uneasy, short tempered, and had even hit her several times. But then he'd apologize and give her extravagant gifts. They hadn't had sex in several weeks. He'd been so withdrawn. She thought that maybe he'd had a lot on his mind. She'd been wanting to have a child and he didn't. Or maybe it was the mortgage, bills, or work stress. She knew that he loved her, but something was definitely bothering him.

Charlotte could never forget the day they met. She was hired as a temp to be Lloyd's secretary. She was sitting in the conference room waiting for Lloyd; it was her first day, and she was very nervous. He walked in and she had immediately lost her train of thought. She hadn't expected her boss to look like that: a handsome bald black man of medium build, probably around 6'1", with a very cocky rather arrogant demeanor.

She had immediately snapped back to attention because she knew this would be interesting. He was talking fast, giving her the rundown of his schedule and his way of doing things. She was most intrigued by his work ethic and his

13

ability and knowledge when it came to investing. He clearly made a lot of money.

They had spent many late nights together working, one night after they ordered dinner in to the office, they had conversed about their personal lives. It was cold that night when they were leaving the office and Charlotte had needed a ride home.

It was dark when they pulled up to her place, and her roommate was gone. As they sat next to each other in the car, Lloyd touched Charlotte's leg. Quietly, she asked, "What are you doing?"

He answered, "What I have always wanted to do." He leaned over and kissed her, hard and deep.

"Slow down," she said, but she asked him to come in anyway.

Suddenly, his hand was between her legs, and she opened up for him with her head pressed back hard against the seat, she slightly raised her hips as he gently inserted his fingers inside her, slowly going in and out , his fingers felt so damn good inside her, as she was moaning and grinding, her body begging for more. She started savagely kissing him, pouring herself out like libation as he made love to her with his fingers, bringing her to complete ecstasy. Lloyd removed his fingers and sucked all her juices from them. That's when she had set her sights on getting this man and marrying him.

These flashback thoughts in the shower turned Charlotte on as the warm water massaged her round succulent breast, she gently grabbed one and started slowly caressing it, and she parted her legs slowly and gently massaging her swollen clit, "the water made it so wet". Charlotte's breathing intensified, as she remembered how Lloyd would make love to her like an animal giving her every inch of him. "It felt so good". Charlotte began, shoving her fingers in and out of her vagina, until she emptied all the passion and desire she longed for.

Lloyd stayed in his study, where he fell asleep and stayed that way until the next morning.

*****

Meanwhile, Diane was sitting in front of her vanity, taking off her earrings.

"Dinner was delicious," she said to Roger.

"Yes, it was," he replied. "But I think Lloyd and Charlotte may be having some problems."

"They seem to be a great couple. Whatever it is, they will work it out."

"I agree. But enough of them—come to bed!" He held the covers open as Diane walked slowly toward him, removing her robe and dirty dancing. Roger smiled and licked his lips, "I've been thinking about you all day."

Diane got on top and straddled Roger. He had a very hard erection, not mention the fact he's very well endowed. She slid his erect cock inside her and moaned, "Mmmmm, it feels so good."

Roger gently caressed her breast while she was slowly grinding on his hard cock. "Ahh," he moaned and groaned, "you're so beautiful."

As he began to go deeper, she said, "Oh baby, this feels so good…I'm about to cum!" He pulled her down to him and started kissing her passionately and deeply. His tongue tasted so good, like whiskey. He continued licking around her lips, he sucked her bottom lip while grinding his cock deep inside her slow, making her orgasm so intense.

Roger flipped her over on her back and spread her legs wide. Roger loved the fact that Diane's good-good was tight, wet, and warm. He always would make a joke that he married her for her good-good.

"Mmmm…" he said, stroking slow and deep, "I love this good-good, this is mine, all mine!"

Through passionate kisses, she answered, "Yes it is baby, all yours!"

Roger passionately whispered in her ear, "That's it; I want us to cum together."

With her legs wide open, Roger began to go deep and slow, "Damn Di."

Diane moaned, "I'm about to cum again, baby."

"Me too, baby, you love this magic stick."

"Yes, I love this magic stick, daddy!"

Roger began to hold her tight, kissing her, sucking her tongue, sucking and licking her breasts, going deeper and deeper. They both started grinding in sync so hard their orgasms were like fireworks. He fell over and they fell fast asleep until the next morning. As Roger was leaving for work, he kissed Diane goodbye.

CHAPTER TWO

That evening, Roger called and said he would be late and not to wait up for him. So Diane decided to pop some popcorn and watch a movie. Sitting on the couch, she saw lights and decided to go take a peek out the window. Outside she saw a car, neither Lloyd's nor Charlotte's; it pulled closer to the back of the house where it was very dark, she could no longer see it. She glanced at the clock; it was 10:00 pm.

All the lights in their house were out except the light in den. Diane wondered who that could be. Still a little curious, she went back to watching her movie. She was thinking it was rather odd that all the lights were out except one. Charlotte and Lloyd didn't have kids, and Charlotte had always kept several lights on when Lloyd was away. Finally, Diane couldn't take it anymore; her curiosity won out. She grabbed her shoes, looked around to make sure no one was watching, and crept over to Charlotte's house.

As Diane was going around to the den window, she could hear light music playing; maybe Charlotte was listening to music. As she approached the window she could see a shadow, and when she got closer she couldn't believe her eyes. Charlotte was on her knees with this random black man's cock in her mouth. After several minutes she got up and turned around, and he shoved his manhood into her. She was saying "Harder!" Diane was so shocked; she slipped slightly and made a noise. Charlotte jumped and pushed the man off her. She came over to the window looking frantic, so Diane ducked down to avoid being seen.

As the guy was scavenging to pull up his pants, Diane could hear Charlotte whisper, "Did you hear that? Hurry up, you have to go!"

"No," he said, not whispering. "Stop being paranoid. You're not finished."

"No," Charlotte said, pushing him toward the door. "You have to go."

That was Diane's cue to hurry back across the street; as she turned to go, she heard the side door open and she jumped behind a tree, her heart beating fast, to hide so Charlotte wouldn't see her. The guy jumped in his car. Diane didn't get the make, model, or tag number—but she definitely saw his face. For some reason he looked familiar, as if she'd seen the guy before, but she wasn't sure.

It seemed to take forever to get back to her house. Once she got in, she stood in the kitchen playing back what she had seen in my mind's eye. Diane knew she couldn't mention this to Roger because he told her mind her business, but it was really beginning to bother her.

*****

A few weeks went by, and Charlotte was doing everything to make sure Lloyd was happy and things were all right between them. Charlotte was in the kitchen cooking dinner before Lloyd came home from work. Lloyd didn't like not having a hot meal after a long day.

She heard his keys in the door signaling that Lloyd was home.

"Hi darling, I'm in the kitchen!"

There was no answer.

"Lloyd, darling, dinner is ready!"

Again, no answer.

Charlotte's back was turned toward the entrance to the kitchen. Out of nowhere, Lloyd grabbed her by her hair and dragged her to the den.

"Lloyd, what are you doing? You're hurting me!" she screamed, crying and kicking at him.

"What am I doing?! What have you been doing?!" he yelled, still dragging her.

"Nothing! What are you talking about?" she cried, trying to get him to release her hair.

"What the hell is this, Charlotte?!" Lloyd held up a condom. "You want to fuck another man in the house I pay for?!"

"What?! I don't know what you're talking about!" Charlotte's fear made her voice crack.

"Charlotte, who's been in my damn house?!"

"No one, Lloyd, I promise!"

Lloyd laughed. "You promise. Charlotte, we don't use condoms!"

"Wait Lloyd, it had to be from the party we had a few weeks ago. I allowed our guests to use the bathroom in the den. Maybe it was one of them. I promise I wouldn't do that to you!"

Charlotte looked at Lloyd, scared that he wouldn't believe her. She thought she'd cleaned everything up. But Lloyd slowly released her hair. Maybe he was thinking it could have been one of the guests; the house had been full, and they couldn't have kept their eyes on everyone. Charlotte had never seen Lloyd this angry. She lay on the floor crying as Lloyd stormed out to his study and slammed the door.

As she slowly peeled herself off the floor, Charlotte assessed her injuries. Her ribs were bruised, and her noise and

21

lip were busted. She was going to have to heal fast before the upcoming promotion party, or she'd have to come up with a convincing story.

CHAPTER THREE

Two weeks had passed and tonight was Web's Investment Firm promotion party. The gathering was hosted in Charlotte and Lloyd's home. Everything was going great. Charlotte ended up speaking to one of Lloyd's investment partners, Ronald Stewart, from Washington, DC most of the night. She was a little tipsy, laughing and gently touching Ronald's shoulder while they were talking. She wasn't aware that Lloyd was watching her from across the room most of night.

After the party was over and the guests left, Charlotte was hanging up her dress in her dressing room. Out of nowhere, Lloyd came in, hauled off, and punched her in the face. She fell into the closet, and he continued to beat her until he got tired. He called her a slut and accused her of coming on to Ronald. That night, she lay on the floor for hours until she managed to get up and drag herself to the bed.

As she was dragging herself across the room, Charlotte's thoughts were interrupted by a vibration sound. It sounded like a phone, which was odd. She slowly tried to move in the direction it was coming from, and she eventually found it in

Lloyd's jacket pocket. She realized that it wasn't Lloyd phone—and the number calling was listed as "private." She wasn't sure why Lloyd had another phone, but she was in too much pain to give a damn at the moment. She put the phone back in his pocket, and put the thoughts about it out of her mind.

*****

Weeks had gone by since Lloyd's episode. Everything was quiet and Lloyd didn't say much. After getting home from work each day, he went straight to his study. That's a relief to Charlotte; she's been staying out of his way. No sooner had she thought that, her phone rings and it's Lloyd.

"Hello?" she said, tentatively.

"Hi, Char."

"Hi…" she said, a little reluctantly.

"I was getting off work early and wanted to take you to dinner."

"I'm not really up to it. Can we have a quiet evening at home?"

There was a beat of silence before Lloyd said, "Sure, that's fine. Is everything all right?"

"Yes," she responded, confused about the direction of the conversation. "I haven't been feeling well lately."

"Ok," he said. "I'm leaving the office shortly; I'm going to grab a movie and something to eat. What do you want to eat?"

"I'm not hungry."

"You sure?"

"Yes."

"Ok, I'll get the movie."

"Ok," she agreed. "See you soon."

Charlotte hung up, thinking it had been a long time since Lloyd spent a Friday night at home. But when she thought about it, she realized that often after one of his outbursts he would wait a few weeks and instead of apologizing he'd get her an expensive gift, a vacation, or a nice dinner. She'd been so tired and exhausted over the past several weeks she was really not in the mood for Lloyd. She heard the door open.

"Baby, where you at?" called Lloyd from the foyer.

"In the family room."

Lloyd walked into the family room and kissed her on the forehead. He handed her the movie he picked out, "White Men Can't Jump." Then he brought his other hand from behind his back, where he was hiding a beautiful bouquet of flowers and a diamond necklace.

"Oh the flowers and the necklace are beautiful! And you got one of our favorite movies—thank you!" Charlotte said, reaching for Lloyd to give him a kiss.

"Yes, I did," he grabbed Charlotte's hand. "I know I haven't been the best husband lately; I've been under so much pressure at work—"

Charlotte interrupted him. "Shh, it's ok. Let's enjoy this night. We haven't had a quiet evening in a long time." She lay her head on his chest, Lloyd gently stroked her hair. They watched the movie, and when it was over, they headed upstairs to bed.

While Charlotte was getting ready for bed, Lloyd told her, "I have to go to DC next week for two weeks."

She walked out the bathroom, putting her hair in a bun to take a shower. "Two weeks? Why two weeks?"

"We're having some issues with a few investors, and they feel it's time for me to step in."

"Can I go with you?"

"No, this is business. There'll be a lot of early and late meetings, and you're going to be bored."

"Ok, I thought it would be nice, since we haven't had much time together."

"I promise when I close this deal, we can go on a long vacation."

Charlotte stepped into the shower, thinking that it had been five months since she and Lloyd had spent time together or even had sex. Her thoughts were interrupted when Lloyd opened the door to the shower and stepped in.

"What are you doing?" she asked?

Turning Charlotte around, Lloyd answered, "What do you think I'm doing? I know what you need." Lloyd slid his erect cock inside her.

"Oh," she moaned, "don't stop!" Right after she said that, Lloyd gave her several pumps and came.

Without saying anything, Lloyd left the shower. As always lately, Charlotte was unsatisfied. She wasn't sure what was going on with Lloyd; he kept getting more and more distant, and she didn't know what to do.

*****

The following week, Charlotte had to drop Lloyd off at the airport around 6:00 pm to catch his flight to DC.

Charlotte yelled upstairs, "Lloyd, are you ready? It's getting late and there's going to be traffic!"

"I can't find my red and blue tie," he yelled back.

"It's in your bottom drawer!"

"Found it—coming."

"Ok, let's go."

As they were heading to the airport, Lloyd was looking at his phone as always, setting up and confirming meetings. Then his phone rang.

He picked up promptly. "Hello, this is Lloyd. How may I help you?

Yes, I'm on my way to the airport; my plane leaves at 7:00 pm." He answered a few more questions and then he hung up the phone.

"Who was that?" Charlotte asked.

"Liz, she was wondering where we were."

"I didn't know Liz was going."

"Yes, I need her so she can keep my schedule together."

"Oh, ok," Charlotte responded, puzzled and pissed.

"What's wrong, Charlotte? This is business. We're not sharing a room!"

"Nothing, be safe."

They kissed goodbye. As Lloyd got out of the car, Liz helped him with his things. They headed off to board their flight.

On the way home, Charlotte couldn't help but think about how she met Lloyd on the job. She was also curious why he never mentioned how gorgeous his new secretary was.

CHAPTER FOUR

It had been several months and Diane and Roger hadn't seen or heard from either Lloyd or Charlotte. Diane never mentioned to Roger what she had seen that night looking through the window, but a few days after the incident she noticed Charlotte coming and going and she was always wearing different shades. Again, it was none of Diane's business. She thought, *Maybe I should call Charlotte later to see if she would like to do lunch this week.*

Shortly after she had that thought, Charlotte pulled into her driveway. Diane waited a few minutes before calling her.

"Hello?" she answered.

"Hi! How are you?"

"I'm fine. I just dropped Lloyd off at the airport."

"Ok," Diane said. "I was going to invite you two to dinner; we haven't seen or heard from you guys in ages."

"I know," she said. "Sorry, Lloyd will be in DC for two weeks, and I'm busy this week. But you and I can get together next week."

"Ok, sure thing. Just let me know."

"Yes definitely, thanks for calling," she said, rushing to get off the phone to put her things down. Charlotte lay her things down in the kitchen and was flooded with tears. As she looked around, she wondered where her happiness went. She could remember how happy she was when Lloyd moved her into their house. The Everglades Estates were newly built. A gated community with a half a million dollar homes. Lloyd said, we were going to the open house to see what they had to offer. When they got there it was two cars in the driveway. The Realtor greeted us at the door and told us to take a look around and she would be with us in just a moment. As we were viewing the bedrooms another couple came out and introduced themselves, it was Roger and Diane. Charlotte fell in love with house. She turned around to tell Lloyd how much she loved the house and he handed her the keys that was the happiest day of her life.

Charlotte's thoughts were interrupted by a call coming in; it was Lloyd.

"Hello," she answered

"Hey Char, wanted to let you know we boarded our flight and I will call you when we get settled in our hotel. I'm tired and I'm going to take a nap before we land."

"Ok, call me when you get settled," she said

"Ok, talk to you later."

Charlotte decided to take a hot bath and a nap to relax her mind. Charlotte didn't realize she slept for two hours until she heard her phone ringing. It was Lloyd letting her know they made it DC safe.

"Hi honey," she answered

"Hey, wanted to check in and let you know we made it safe, so you wouldn't be worried."

She said, "Good. What's your schedule looking like?"

"We're meeting tonight at Bar-None for drinks and to discuss our next move," Lloyd told her.

"Ok," she said. "Don't work too hard, get some rest, and call me when you're free."

"Ok, talk to you later," he said. She could hear a knock at the door through the phone.

Lloyd opened the door to see Liz standing there, wearing a form-fitting dress that showed off her thick thighs, big ass, and nice, round tits. Liz was black, and her body was basically the opposite of Charlotte's skinny frame.

"Boss, we have a meeting at Bar-None in an hour," she said, standing in the doorway.

"I know,' he said, "Let me get a shower and change first."

As Liz walked away down the hotel hallway, Lloyd gave a long, appreciative look at her body in that dress. As he shut the door, he thought, *Damn, stay focused*!

The meeting went well at Bar-None. Everyone got a little tipsy, and Lloyd noticed Liz and Ronald having a good time and laughing. For some reason it made him feel jealous.

He went over to where they were standing near the bar. "I'm about to turn in," he said. "We have a long day tomorrow."

"It's early, boss. Everything ok?"

"Yes, I'm just tired."

"Ok," she said. "Get some rest; I'm going to be another hour before I turn in."

"Ok—and Ronald, take good care of her," Lloyd said before heading for the door.

"No problem, boss, I got her," Ronald called after him.

Back at the hotel, as Lloyd was heading to his room, his phone rang. "Yes, give me ten minutes. I'm in room 211."

Ten minutes later, there was a knock at the door. Lloyd answered it with a towel wrapped around his waist. This time, standing in the doorway was his boy toy, James. James and Lloyd had been on the DL for a long time. They met in college and they had been on and off for over twenty years.

In Lloyd's mind, he wasn't gay. But Charlotte had no idea about Lloyd's lifestyle. He certainly planned to keep it a secret—it would be unacceptable to his family, friends, and colleagues.

"Come in," he said to James. "I don't have much time."

James immediately grabbed Lloyd's erect cock and dropped to knees to take Lloyd's full manhood in his mouth.

Lloyd held James's head and shoved his manhood deeper into his mouth. "Oh shit, I missed this. I like the way you take all my ten inches in your mouth." After Lloyd impregnated James's mouth, he turned him around and started shoving his manhood in him

"Lloyd, slow down, it hurts," James said. It seemed like Lloyd didn't hear him, so he repeated, "Lloyd! Slow down! You're hurting me!"

Lloyd kept ramming James as if he was angry, and James pulled away abruptly.

Lloyd snapped back to the present like his thoughts were interrupted. "What's wrong?"

James said, "Didn't you hear me? What's wrong with you? Why are you hurting me?!"

Lloyd suddenly grabbed James by his throat. "Don't you ever question me," he snarled in James's face.

"Let go, Lloyd, you're hurting me! What did I do wrong?"

Lloyd pushed James away. "Nothing. Bye, man, just go," Lloyd said as he started putting on his briefs and night pants.

James walked out the door still fixing his pants just as Liz was entering her room. She noticed James leaving Lloyd's room, and she was puzzled. She looked at her watch; it was 3:00 am.

*****

A week went by, and Charlotte didn't hear much from Lloyd. She had come to expect that when he went out of town, since he was busy and had to get a lot done before returning home.

Liz called him on his hotel phone. "Hey boss, you have two meetings this week, and I booked our flight for Friday."

"Sure thing. And Liz, can you send my wife some flowers?"

"Sure, boss," Liz said, a flashback of the man leaving Lloyd's room late at night going through her mind.

"Thank you. I'll see you later."

*****

Charlotte was sitting in the sun room when the doorbell rang.

"May I help you," she said when she opened the door and saw a delivery man standing there.

"I have a delivery for Charlotte, please sign here," he said.

"That's me," she said as she signed. "Thank you."

Charlotte took the flowers to the kitchen to read the card. They were from Lloyd. The card said that he missed me and he loved her. Shaking her head, she thought, *Every time Lloyd makes a mistake I receive flowers, a vacation, or nice expensive gifts.* But she couldn't understand why, if he loved her, he continued to hurt her. Several minutes later, Charlotte heard her phone receive a text.

It was Donte, asking, "Do you have panties on?"

Charlotte giggled and texted back, "No."

"I'm on my way, I'll be there at 11:00 pm," he responded.

"Park down the street and flash your light twice so I know it's you," she instructed him. "When I turn off the porch light, then you come to the side door."

Charlotte ran upstairs to shower and put on something more comfortable. Several minutes later, Donte texted her that he'd just parked. She turned off the porch light and met him at the side door. Charlotte took him by the hand and led him to the basement. She needed to be more careful. Lloyd barely ever went down there anymore.

"Are you ok," Donte asked her. "Why are we going to the basement?"

"We have to be more careful," she replied. "Lloyd found condoms in the den behind the trash can last time."

Charlotte sat Donte on the couch and started massaging the shaft of his penis, tastefully spitting on it for wetness. Before she knew it, she was riding his young cock like she was in a rodeo. She came so hard she fell over, exhausted.

"We're not finished," Donte told her. "Come here and suck it to get it harder."

Charlotte dropped to her knees and started sucking and slurping on Donte's young massive cock until it was hard as a rock. The he turned Charlotte on her stomach, slowly penetrating her, taking his time slowly going in and out. Charlotte was moaning and groaning. Donte came so hard and started banging her until the condom was full of cum. But it was getting late and it was time for Donte to go.

"Donte, you have to go," she said, putting her robe back on.

"Why can't I stay? Your husband won't be home for a few days."

"You can't stay. Please, you have to go."

Donte looked Charlotte in the eyes. "We've been doing this for two years. I know your husband isn't treating you right because you have told me over and over…"

"Look, it's complicated. You and I are friends, right?" she asked, holding his face in her hands.

"No, it's not complicated. Just leave him. I love you, Charlotte."

Charlotte was shocked. "Donte, you don't love me. You have to go."

Donte was confused by her response. "Did I say something wrong? Ok, wait, I'm sorry."

"No, please go," she pleaded. "We can't do this anymore. You have your life ahead of you and you're ten years younger than me. Donte, we can't be together."

Donte grabbed Charlotte by the arm and yanked her. "You don't say I'm too young when I'm banging your brains out and you're sucking on my dick!"

"Donte, let me go! It's time for you to go!"

"I'm sorry, Charlotte, but I love you and I want to be with you. I can't do this anymore." He walked over to Charlotte and started grabbing her and kissing her very hard as Charlotte tried to pull away.

"Donte, stop please!" she begged as Donte kissed all over her neck passionately. Finally, Charlotte couldn't resist any longer, and she dropped her robe. Donte lay her back on the couch and put his face between her legs. With every deep breath Charlotte took, Donte's tongue gently licked and sucked and nibbled on her clit, and it drove her crazy.

"Cum in my mouth, Charlotte, I want to drink your passion!"

"Yes, baby," she moaned.

Donte started gently pushing his tongue in and out of her vagina. She grabbed his head and started grinding so hard; she released all her juices in his mouth, and he drank every bit of it.

When Donte came up for air, Charlotte grabbed his face to kiss him and suck all her juices off his tongue. That drove Donte crazy.

*****

The next morning, while preparing her coffee, Charlotte couldn't help but think about the previous night. This fling between her and Donte had gone too far; she should have ended it a year ago. She thought, *Donte can't love me. I'm married and I told him I wasn't leaving my husband.* But Donte was dark dipped in chocolate; he was young, hot, handsome, and very well endowed—much bigger than Lloyd. He had so much more stamina and he gave her great head for hours if she wanted it. Donte's desire was to please her. Lloyd used to be that way with her, but now over the last three years, things had changed.

Charlotte had been so broken, confused, and abused the day she met Donte. Lloyd had taken so much from her, and Donte gave her so much attention. He made her feel beautiful and wanted again; it was like an awakening. Donte was only twenty-five years old, ten years younger than Charlotte. He worked at the grocery store that everyone frequented in the neighborhood. That particular day Charlotte couldn't reach the marinade, and Donte came over to help. He was 6'2" and broad; she could tell by looking at him that he played football in high school and college. They had talked a little, and she was impressed by how mature and intelligent he was.

A week later, Charlotte went to the store for a few things for dinner, and she had seen him there again. He said he did handy work on the side, and he gave her his number. She was very curious and took the number but was very reluctant to call. Some time passed and the hurt Charlotte suffered from Lloyd piled up. One day at the store Donte noticed there was something wrong with her. He acted very concerned and consoled her. She ended up crying in his arms and it had felt so damn good. Later that night Charlotte called to just talk.

One thing led to another, and now two years later it was still going on. She cared for Donte, but she loved Lloyd.

CHAPTER FIVE

That night, Roger would be accepting an award from Time Out Magazine for DJ of the year. There was an award party every year, and Roger had won the last two years. Earlier that day, Diane picked up her dress and his suit. Roger actually made it home on time tonight—Diane couldn't believe it.

Roger was running up the stairs, undressing to get changed for the party. "Diane, you ready?"

"Yes," she replied, putting on her diamond earrings. "Hurry so we won't be late!"

Roger kissed her on the back of her neck. "Mmmm, you look so sexy in that dress." He pulled her gently to him, nibbling on her ear.

Blushing and playfully pulling away, she said, "Thanks, but not now. Roger. We have to go." But he could tell from her tone that she was giving in.

"Come on, let's have a quickie. I will make it quick."

Laughing and kissing him gently on the lips, she said, "No, we have to go. You can get all you want later tonight."

Roger laughed with her, "Ok, I thought I would try." Turning around to fix his tie in the mirror, he said, "I'm ready."

Diane called him over to adjust his tie. "There you go. You look so hot and handsome. I'm proud of you."

Roger kissed her and said, "Thank you—and I can't wait to get you out this dress!"

"I can't wait either."

When they arrived at the award ceremony there were so many people there; it was a red carpet affair. Everyone was taking pictures; Roger and Diane were a picture-perfect couple. Inside they did the meet and greet, and then they led them to their table. They were seated with a few other DJs from the area and some from other states. Diane ordered a martini and Roger ordered a shot of Jack Daniels. They ordered their meals and ate as the ceremony started. There was a lot of laughter and chit chat with their tablemates, and by the time Roger received the DJ of year award, they were very tipsy. Then they turned up the music and the party started.

After several hours Diane was across the room sipping her martini. She looked up and noticed the conversation between Roger and this nice looking white girl. Diane had never seen her before, but Roger seemed a little uneasy. Diane didn't think anything of it, so she turned around to finish her drink and conversation. Then later she turned around to order another drink, and didn't see Roger anywhere in sight. A few minutes later he surfaced from outside, and Diane walked over to him.

She rubbed his arm, and Roger put his arm around her waist. "Everything all right, DJ of the Year?" He laughed and gently kissed her on the lips. "Yes, why do you ask?"

"Just making sure. You're a little drunk."

Roger leaned in with the strong smell of whiskey on his breath. "I'm good, I'm ok."

"Ok," Diane said, reassured. "Let me go say hi to Misty."

Misty was Roger's executive assistant; she had been with Roger for many years. She handled all his affairs, arranging his flights, radio show appearances, TV interviews, and so on. While Diane was talking to Misty, she noticed that the gentlemen from the front door walked over to Roger, whispered something in his ear, and led Roger out into the corridor. The gentlemen led Roger to a side area, and when Roger looked over to the corner, he saw Tabatha.

"Roger, can we talk?" she said, moving toward him.

Through clenched teeth, Roger said, "No!" and grabbed Tabatha by the arm, dragging her into a different side room.

"What the hell are you doing here? Didn't I tell you, you have to go. My wife is here!"

"Roger, why are treating me this way? You just stopped calling and you changed your number."

"Treating you like what, the whore that you are?" Roger's barely contained anger showed in his voice, although he was keeping himself from yelling. "You knew what it was. I told you I was married and I was not leaving my wife. What we had was over a year ago!"

Tabatha laughed devilishly, "Oh, so you're not leaving your black bitch wife? Did she know about us when she was on her tours and you couldn't make it? Did she know where you were? Your precious wife would be brokenhearted if she knew the things you were doing to me while she was out of town!"

"Don't you ever call my wife a black bitch again or I will—" he was so angry he raised his fist to bash her face but then decided against it. As he was walking off, he said, "You better be gone by the time I leave this room. Stay away from me and my wife, or else!"

As soon as Roger re-entered the main party room, Diane headed his way.

"Hey, is everything ok? I was looking for you."

"Yes," he said. "Let's go, I'm beat."

44

"Are you sure?" she asked. "The night is still young."

"Yes, I'm tired."

"Ok, let me get my things. Are you sure you're ok?"

"Yes Di, everything is ok."

"Ok," she said, giving him a peck on his lips.

Roger helped Diane with her coat and they headed out the door to go home. Diane noticed that Roger was very withdrawn on the way home. He usually talked about the night, but that night something was bothering him. She decided not to pursue it, since he'd told her at the party that everything was fine. Once they got home Roger headed straight upstairs, and a few minutes later she was behind him. He was in the shower when she got upstairs.

While in the shower, Roger let the hot water run over his head. Roger couldn't stop recalling the incident with Tabatha and the mistake he had made. He had met Tabatha at The Doll House, a gentlemen's club, a year ago. Diane had been on tour a lot, and when Roger found out that they only had a 50/50 chance of having child after trying for so many years, he was devastated, and he would go out and drink with the guys on occasion. One night while at the The Doll House he was very drunk; the music came on and out came Tabatha. She was built like a black woman and her ass was natural. She had fake tits but Roger was like Damn, she bad. He loved Diane and had never had a desire for another woman. Although Roger was white, he had always been attracted to black women.

That night, his buddies dared him to go into the back room and get a private dance. He did it, but he didn't know about the extra shit. Tabatha was dancing all over him and he was drunk. It was feeling good; he grabbed Tabatha and felt his second head get hard. Roger was usually in control but with the liquor, the music, and her body all oiled up, he didn't stop her when she gently massaged the bulge that was swelling up in his pants. Before he knew it his pants were slightly down by his waist and his second head was peeking through the hole in the front of his boxers. As he was sitting in the chair she slid the second head inside her and started slowly riding, leaning forward with her breast in his face, the sweet fragrance had him in a drug-induced haze. Her warm breathing deeply on his neck with every gasp. His hands were all over this girl and he was shoving his cock all inside her. Just as he realized what he was doing, he came.

That night he had gone home so ashamed, but the shame didn't last long because he started calling Tabatha. They would meet out and have sex when Diane would go out of town. Roger ended it when he started noticing Tabatha was getting clingy and pushy. He just stopped calling her. Then she would call and he blocked her number. Eventually, Roger changed his number. It had been a year since he saw her and he would not let her ruin his life.

Roger stepped out the shower and his phone was vibrating.

"Hello?"

"Roger." It was Tabatha.

In a whisper, Roger said, "How did you get my damn number?!"

"Roger, we need to talk."

"We have nothing to talk about. Stop calling my phone."

Diane walked into the bathroom. "Who were you talking to?"

"No one, it was a wrong number," Roger said as he kissed her forehead.

*****

Charlotte looked at her watch. It was 4:30 pm—time to leave. Lloyd's flight was arriving at 6:00 pm. As Charlotte pulled up to the terminal, she was still a bit disturbed by Donte; she knew it was time to cut things off with him as soon as possible. She thought maybe it would be better to text Donte instead of meeting with him to break it off. But her husband's flight had just landed and she had to go in to greet him. Lloyd was at the baggage claim.

She waved and called out to him. "Lloyd, honey, over here!"

Lloyd looked up and headed Charlotte's way. He kissed and hugged her. "Oh, it's so good to be home."

"Yes," she agreed. "I'm glad you're home. I missed you."

When they arrived home, Lloyd dropped his bags at the door and went straight to his study. Exhausted, he closed the door sat in his chair with his head back and eyes closed. Lloyd hadn't been answering James's calls. He thought back to the day that he and James had met.

It was twenty years ago in college. James was a waiter at this hole-in-the-wall bar that all the basketball players used hang out at to watch the game and wind down. James was very attentive to Lloyd like a bitch; he could usually identify who's down. There's nothing gay about James; Lloyd was more into gay DL (down low) brothers. James is 45 years old and in private Lloyd calls him his "boy toy." If someone saw them out on a "business lunch" they would look like two men meeting for drinks. No one would suspect that James is gay when talking to him. He had the same problem as Lloyd— because of their families and Lloyd's position, they couldn't come out, but that was changing for James.

Lloyd had thought this arrangement would work, but his world was complicated and James wanted more. James also mentioned moving to New York. Lloyd could go for several months and even a year at times before the thirst overpowered him. He had tried several times to break it off with James, but James had tried several times to kill himself. Lloyd's perfect world would be to have Charlotte and James, but he couldn't have that. It got hard sometimes and he would take it out on Charlotte. Lloyd loved Charlotte, but James quenched that thirst in him. He could do things to James that he couldn't do with Charlotte, but he had to cut this off with him. Lloyd's phones started vibrating; he looked down and saw it was James. Lloyd pressed ignore and turned his phone off. He put it in the top draw of his desk and went to bed.

CHAPTER SIX

It was the end of the summer and Diane couldn't believe they hadn't taken a trip with Lloyd and Charlotte that year. Everyone was so busy and distracted. She thought of trying to plan a weekend trip for the four of them and called Charlotte to talk about it.

"Hi, Charlotte," Diane said when she picked up. "Long time no hear!"

Charlotte laughed. "I know. How are you?"

"I'm great. I wanted to see if you and Lloyd were free next weekend for a quiet weekend at the lake house—and we're not taking no for an answer!"

"Well, if that's the case, then yes, we will join the two of you," Charlotte replied.

"Great! I will call and make the arrangements. See you guys next weekend!"

As soon as Charlotte hung up she immediately called Lloyd to ask what his schedule was like the next weekend.

"I'm free," he said. "What's up?"

"Diane and Roger want us to go with them to the lake house."

"That's great," Lloyd said. "We haven't been away in months; that would be nice to get away."

"Ok, good!" She smiled to herself, excited at the idea. "I already told Diane yes."

"Anything for you."

Charlotte hung up, still smiling. Lately Lloyd had been home early, had no late meetings and he hadn't been abusive. She wondered how long this would last. She'd noticed Lloyd's phone ringing a lot more than usual, but she didn't care as long as things were going well. She didn't want to ruin the moment.

*****

While Diane was setting the table, Roger walked in and kissed her on the back of her head.

"Something smells good," he said, headed to the refrigerator.

"You're favorite: homemade lasagna, a beautiful tossed salad, Texas toast breadsticks, and a bottle of red wine."

"Oh baby," Roger said, rubbing his stomach, "I'm hungry."

As they sat down to eat, Diane said, "I forgot to tell you, I made plans for me, you, Lloyd, and Charlotte to go to the lake house next weekend."

Through a forkful of food in his mouth, Roger asked, "Have you talked to Lloyd and Charlotte?"

"Yes, and they said yes. I also called the groundskeeper and he's going to clean up next Wednesday. He's going to change the linens, and I sent him a grocery list. Everything is taken care of."

"Wow Di, you covered everything! This is great; we definitely need a break away from here."

Diane reached over and covered Roger's hand with mine. "Yes, we do. You seem so distracted lately, and we need some alone time. The nature will do us some good too."

"I agree," Roger was saying when his phone started to vibrate. He glanced down at it and it was a text from Tabatha: "911." Roger thought, *What does this bitch want?* On his face it showed that he was annoyed and distracted.

Diane was cleaning the table and she asked, "Who was that?"

No answer.

"Roger?"

Snapping out his trance, Roger said "Yes?"

"I asked who that was"

"I'm not sure," he said. "I will call them back later."

Diane walked into the kitchen and thought she saw a shadow. In fright, she dropped the glasses.

Roger jumped up and came running into the kitchen. "Di, you ok?" He started helping her pick up the broken glass.

"Yes. I thought I saw a shadow outside, but I think it was my shadow in the window. Silly me."

"Di, you're tired. Go up and get some rest; I'll finish cleaning this up."

"Ok, thank you honey," she said, giving him a kiss.

"Ok, I will be up shortly."

Roger waited for her to head upstairs, and then he went to take the trash out so he could call Tabatha. He didn't want to believe that Tabatha followed him home. When he called her, she picked up right away, laughing.

"You think this is funny?" he said. "I warned you to stay away from wife and my home!"

"Do you think you can do whatever you want to me and get away with it?" she said.

"I didn't do anything to you. We had sex several times, that's it, that's all."

"No, Roger!" she said angrily crying. "You called me—you used me!"

"You're a crazy psycho bitch! Don't make me—"

"Make you what, Roger? If you don't meet me Friday to talk, I will tell your wife everything."

"Look, I will meet you next week. I can't meet you Friday."

"This Friday!" she said. "Or else!"

Roger tried to appease her. "Ok, ok, look, I will try. What time Friday?"

"At 7:00 pm meet me at the Four Seasons Hotel on Madison. I will text you with the room number."

"Ok, I will be there". He hung up immediately and went back into the house.

When Roger got upstairs, Diane was on her laptop. "Di, what time are we leaving Friday?"

"8:00 pm."

"Ok," Roger replied, wishing he hadn't gotten himself into this mess. He needed to figure how he could meet Tabatha and be home on time for the trip Friday. But he was determined to do whatever it took to keep Tabatha away from Diane.

*****

It was 6:00 pm on Friday Diane was excited about the upcoming trip to the lake house. She had spoken to Roger earlier, and he said he had an emergency with one of his DJs and he needed to handle some business. She tried calling him, but there was no answer, so she finished packing their things. She checked her watch and it was 7:15. She wondered where Roger was.

It was 7:00 by the time Roger got to the hotel. Tabatha texted him the room number: 510. Roger took the elevator to fifth floor and knocked on the door.

Tabatha opened the door in a see-through nightgown. She threw the door open and walked straight toward the couch. Roger thought her ass was looking good but he needed to get rid of this crazy bitch for good.

"Hurry up. What do we need to talk about? I have another meeting to get to."

Tabatha walked toward Roger. "I've been thinking about you, us," she said, as she reached for him.

Roger pushed her hands away. "I don't have time for your games. Look, Tabatha, there's no us I'm sorry. I love my wife, and I shouldn't have done what I did with you."

"Sorry!" Tabitha screamed. "Yes you're sorry—a sorry son of a bitch!" She started crying angry tears.

"Look, calm down. What do you want to talk about?"

"Calm down! Who else have you done this to?"

"No one! Just leave me alone! This is my last time telling you!" he yelled as he headed for the door.

Tabatha was on her knees, crying and grabbing Roger's shirt. "I love you! I fell in love with you!"

Roger grabbed both of her wrists hard. Look, you crazy bitch: I don't love you, I never did love you. You were a side a piece of ass and it wasn't all that great. As you said, "I love black coffee, no sugar, no cream." He shoved her to the floor and stormed out.

Roger looked at his watch; it was 7:45. He had ten missed calls from Diane. He calmed himself down, waited fifteen minutes, and called her back.

"Hello, where are you?" she said, sounding a little puzzled.

"Hey Di, I'm around the corner, I'll be pulling up shortly. I told the guys they couldn't keep me long because you had a trip planned and they let me go." He laughed.

"Ok," she said. "We're waiting for you. See you shortly."

Roger hung up, relieved to have made it by the skin of his teeth. Tabatha was stressing him out and something had to be done.

*****

The first night at the lake house they had a nice dinner. They roasted marshmallows, played games, and drank plenty of booze. The second day was spent out on the boat most of the day. When they got back to the lake house at dusk, Charlotte went to bed early since she said she was lightheaded and wasn't feeling well. Lloyd took his laptop to the deck to do some work, and Roger and Diane went for a walk through the woods. When they got back they thought everyone was sleep. Diane checked on Charlotte; she was sleep and Lloyd was still on the deck working.

Diane stuck her head outside. "Goodnight, Lloyd."

She noticed that Lloyd was on his phone, but couldn't hear what he was talking about. It seemed serious.

Lloyd put his hand over the phone. "Goodnight, Diane."

Roger and Diane headed up stairs to their room. When Diane shut the door, Roger grabbed her hand and gently laid her on the bed.

"Mmmm," Diane said in her sexy voice. "What are you doing?"

"What I enjoy doing to you." Laying on top of her, looking her in the eyes intimately and gently kissing her lips. "You know I love you."

"Yes, I know you love me. And I love you more," Diane said, smiling.

"Don't ever question my love for you,"

"I don't, baby." He was kissing, licking, and sucking her bottom lip gently, and it drove her crazy.

Roger slid his erect one-eyed monster in her and made love to her like never before. They had a wonderful sex life. Diane had never imagined a white boy being as big as Roger was, and it was so good. Yes, Diane thought the one-eyed monster was good, but that night was different, it was as if Roger was making love to her soul, wanting to tell her something.

*****

On the way home from the lake house they were talking, singing, and having a great time discussing when to plan their next getaway. As they pulled into the driveway, they couldn't believe their eyes. Someone had spray painted "Nigger Lover" on the side of Roger and Diane's house. Roger jumped out the car, outraged. Diane got out the car in shock, and walking up close to read the red writing.

Charlotte was also outraged. "Who would do such a thing?"

"I don't know," said Lloyd, "but I'm calling the police."

Roger hugged Diane, pulling her close and holding her tightly.

"We've been in this neighborhood for ten years and this has never happened," she said.

"I know, Di. I'm sorry."

"Roger, you have nothing to be sorry about. The bastards who did this are sorry! I'm going to find out who did this, and they will pay." Outraged and disappointed, she walked into the house.

The police arrived shortly after. The officer in charge asked, "Do you know anyone who would do something like this? A jealous girlfriend or boyfriend?"

Outraged by the question, Diane said, "No, sir!"

Roger held Diane around her shoulders. "No, sir, we have lived here for ten years. Everyone in the neighborhood knows us, and we have never had any problems in this community, not even a break-in."

The police officer handed Roger a copy of the report. "If you see any suspicious activity, please call us."

Everyone hugged and said good night, and Roger and Diane headed into the house. Lloyd and Charlotte got their bags out of the car and walked across the street to go home.

Diane was very quiet and withdrawn as Roger walked up behind her in her dressing room.

Rubbing her shoulders, he asked, "Are you ok?"

"Yes, people are mean and hurtful. I love everyone and I treat people right. What did we do to deserve this?"

Roger interrupted her. "Listen, Di, you didn't do anything." He held her face in his hands.

"I know. When I find out who did this, they will see the DC side of me they didn't want to see."

Roger giggled at the thought, "They don't know what they're up against."

*****

Charlotte took her bags straight to her room. She still wasn't feeling well and hadn't been lately.

"I feel so bad for Diane," she said. "To come home and see that spray painted on your house!"

"Yes, I agree. And the cowards will pay for what they did. You know they messed with the wrong one; Diane is from the hood and she's made a great life for herself. She don't play—that's why Roger is in line."

Charlotte chuckled. "Yes, she's so loving—but don't get her wrong," she said. She was already slightly dozing off.

"I have some emails to check, you get some rest."

Lloyd went to the bathroom to undress, and by the time he came out of the bathroom Charlotte was fast asleep. That was good, because Lloyd needed to call James after James had told him he may be moving to New York.

"What's up," Lloyd said when James answered the phone.

"I just wanted you know that I now live here in New York."

Lloyd was angry. "I thought we discussed that this would not be a good idea."

"Well I don't see you enough, and now I can see more of you," James said.

"No, you can't. Look, James, it's time we called it quits. I can't risk Charlotte finding out about us."

"No, Lloyd, please," James begged. "I promise not to interfere or cause trouble! Can you stop by later this week so we can talk?"

"I will let you know," Lloyd said. "I have to go."

*****

Roger didn't sleep all night; he tossed and turned because he knew the only person who could have done this was Tabatha. It was time he paid her a visit. Roger tried calling her phone but she didn't answer, so he texted her.

"We need to talk, ASAP."

She didn't answer.

CHAPTER SEVEN

A few weeks had passed since the incident, and Roger hadn't heard from Tabatha. Roger decided to see if he could find Tabatha's address on Peoplelocator. He had forgotten her last name, so he called the club pretending to be someone else. The young lady who answered the phone seemed to become irritated when he asked for Tabatha.

"Doll House, this is Kay. How may I help you?"

"May I speak to Tabatha please?" Roger asked.

Kay paused, breathing hard. "Which one—white Tabatha or black Tabatha?"

"White Tabatha," Roger chuckled. "I apologize, I forgot her last name."

"Oh, it's Tabatha McCarthy. She isn't working today. Actually, she hasn't been in all week. Can I take a message?"

"No that's all right; thank you."

Roger went back to the website and entered Tabatha's full name. All her information popped up: address, name, age, the last few places she'd lived, and—BAM—her current address.

*****

Charlotte hadn't spoken to Diane since they returned from the trip so she decided to give her a call.

"Hi girl," she said. "How are you?"

"I'm great," Diane responded. "Thanks for asking. I've been talking with my publisher, and she said it's time I get back on track. It's been a year since my last book. How are you? Lloyd mentioned you haven't been feeling well."

"Yes, I think I've been extremely tired. But I feel 1,000% better today."

"Good! We have to get together and have dinner, just the two of us."

"Yes, I need that. Let me know when you're available. Oh, and do you guys have any info on the vandalizer?"

"Nope, no one saw anything. But I will catch you up when we meet."

"Ok good, talk to you later."

Charlotte hung up and tried calling Lloyd, but he didn't answer. Charlotte hadn't talked to Donte in weeks; she'd blocked his number. She once thought she saw him drive past the house, but it wasn't him. She couldn't avoid him any longer but she didn't want to lead him on. Things were getting very complicated. Charlotte got dressed to go get a few things at the grocery store. She scanned the parking lot and didn't see any sign of Donte or his car. It was Wednesday and she knew that was his day off.

As she was shopping, she turned right to go down the aisle, and she ran head-on into another cart.

"Oh! Excuse me, I'm so sorry. I wasn't paying attention." She looked up to see who she had crashed into and saw it was a handsome black man.

"No, excuse me," he said, looking Charlotte up and down.

As Charlotte went down the next aisle she thought about how handsome he was. Her thoughts were interrupted when she ran into him again.

"We keep running into each other," he said. "Maybe you should give me your number so I can make you dinner."

Charlotte smiled and looking away. "No, I'm sorry, I'm married." She walked past him to reach for some rice.

"I got that," he said, extending his hand. "My name is James. What's yours?"

"Charlotte."

"Charlotte, I know you said you're married, but can we be friends?"

"It was nice to meet you, James, but I have to go," she said, walking away.

"Wait," he said. "I apologize. I understand, and sorry to bother you."

Charlotte had a weakness for handsome black men. She found herself curious as to what she could get away with, and it was time she broke it off with Donte. Charlotte checked out, and James watched her walk to her car. She was putting her bags in the car when James walked up to help her.

She thanked him and he smiled. "You're welcome. Have a nice day."

Charlotte got in her car and headed home. She thought about James on her way home, and couldn't get him off her mind. Once she got home and started putting things away, she reached into the bag and pulled out a business card with James's number on it. He was a consultant. She smirked, thinking how he must have dropped it in her bag when he helped her put them in the car.

James watched Charlotte drive away and couldn't believe how easy it had been to approach her. He'd been following Charlotte for weeks, putting his plan together. She was the reason he and Lloyd couldn't be together. James had been in the closet for so many years, and Lloyd was the first and only guy he'd slept with. He loved him. Lloyd had said he was going to leave her for James three years ago. Now he'd been ignoring James's calls and he wanted to break it off. That's what he thought, but Lloyd would pay for doing James that way.

*****

Roger had been on a personal rampage trying to find Tabatha, and after several weeks, as he was parked across from her apartment, he saw her getting out of someone's car. He waited a few minutes after she went in building and then called her.

"What do you want?!"

"We need to talk," Roger said.

"Now you want to talk. About what? I'm busy."

"You know what I want to talk about, just me and you. I will be there in fifteen minutes."

"Fifteen minutes," she said. "You don't know where I live!"

"I can always find you," Roger said and then hung up.

Tabatha jumped in the shower. Her doorbell rang a few minutes later, and when she opened the door Roger charged at her. He grabbed her around her neck, choking her so hard she couldn't breathe. She was struggling to break loose, but when Roger realized she was losing consciousness he let her go and walked out her apartment while Tabatha was still coughing and grasping for air.

Roger was unmoved and unbothered as he got in his car to go home. *I should have killed that bitch*, he thought. He tried calling Diane, but there was no answer.

When Roger got home Diane had her earphones in and she was typing on her laptop. Coming up behind and her kissing her on the back of her head, he said, "Hi, I was calling you."

Diane removed her headphones. "Sorry, I got a call from my publisher, and they need this manuscript by the end of the year."

"Good, Di. I didn't realize it's been a year already."

Diane smiled. "Yeah, yeah, yeah. How was your day?"

"It was boring. I had several meetings; there's a new night club opening and they want us on a contract for the first year."

"That's great. Are you going to sign?"

"Yeah, with a few minor demands. I'm not sure who I'm going to put in the booth. Anyway, I'm going up to shower—I'm tired."

"I will be up shortly," she said, turning back to her laptop.

In the shower Roger kept recalling what happen at Tabatha's house. All he could think was that he wished he had killed her.

*****

Lloyd was on his way home from work when his phone rang. It was James.

"What's up?" James asked.

"Nothing," Lloyd answered, his tone vague.

"Can you stop by please so we can talk?"

"James, look—"

"No, Lloyd! I need to see you tonight, and we need to talk. I've been patient with you for twenty years. You told me you were going to leave your wife, and you didn't. All the lies and the sneaking around—I'm done with it! Or since you don't want to talk to me, how about I talk to your wife?

Lloyd was silent, mad as hell, thinking, Why did I even get involved with this dude?

"James, look, you're right. We have to talk. Let me make a few calls and I will call you back.

As soon as he hung up, he called Charlotte to tell her he would have a late meeting that night and not to wait up for him.

"Oh Lloyd, I cooked dinner. We haven't had a quiet evening since our weekend vacation a month ago."

"I know, and I'm sorry. I will try to wrap things up quickly."

Charlotte said, "Ok, see you later." But she thought to herself, Another night alone.

Charlotte reached into her robe pocket and pulled out James's number. She was nervous as the phone rang.

"Hello, hello," he said.

"Hi James, this is Charlotte."

"Charlotte, hi! How are you? I thought you would never call since I gave you my number weeks ago."

"I know—and I don't know why I called."

"Well I'm glad you called; I'm assuming your husband isn't home."

"Maybe I shouldn't have called. I have to go."

"Charlotte, wait—sorry! I just want to be friends. What's a gorgeous sexy woman like you doing home alone?

Charlotte giggled. "My husband is working late again tonight."

"If I was your husband, I wouldn't leave you home alone. I would want you with me at all times."

"Well, you're not my husband, and I'm home alone."

"Yeah, well, when can I cook for you?"

Charlotte laughed. "Cook for me? No one has ever cooked for me."

"Well I would like to cook for you Friday night, if you can get away."

"I'm not sure about that, but I will let you know."

"Ok, Charlotte, you do that and I look forward to possibly seeing you." His phone beeped, signaling a call on the other line. "Can you hold on?"

"Sure."

James clicked over to the other line. It was Lloyd.

"I'm on my way," he said. "I will be there around 10:30 pm."

"Ok."

James clicked back to Charlotte. "I'm back, sweetness. Look, I have to go. Let me know what you want to do and I will prepare dinner Friday."

"Ok, nice talking to you," Charlotte said.

*****

71

Lloyd arrived at James's apartment. James opened the door in his briefs and a t-shirt.

"Hey," he said to Lloyd.

Lloyd closed the door behind him, and turning around he couldn't help but watch James walk to the couch. *Stay focused!* he thought, but he hadn't had a piece of ass in weeks. He needed to relieve some stress out on this bitch.

"So, Lloyd, where are we going with us?" James asked, sitting across from Lloyd.

"James, why have 'us' and what we have become so complicated? We both agreed. You knew I was married—"

"But Lloyd, you said you didn't love her anymore and you thought she was cheating on you."

"James, you know we can't let anyone know about us."

"Lloyd, I love you and I want to be with you!" He got up and went over to sit next to Lloyd, rubbing Lloyd's leg.

"James, please stop," Lloyd said, moving James's hand away.

James scooted closer, grabbing Lloyd's cock. "I know you want some."

"James, man, we can't keep doing this," Lloyd protested, fighting the temptation.

James was overpowering Lloyd's willpower. "No, don't you miss this ass?"

"James, look, I have to go. I came by to let you know it's over." He was trying to stand up with a half-erect penis.

"Mmmhmm, it's getting hard. Don't fight it; we will never be over."

"James, please, I have to go." He was breathing hard, trying to fight, but it was feeling so damn good.

"No," James said, pushing Lloyd back on the couch and slowly unbuttoning his pants. "Don't fight it."

Lloyd lay back with his eyes closed and James pulled out his erect penis. It was so hard.

James was on his knees in front of Lloyd. Lloyd stopped fighting and watched as James shoved all ten inches of his erect penis in his mouth. Lloyd liked it when James took all of his manhood deep in his mouth. Lloyd couldn't treat Charlotte the way he treated James. Lloyd grabbed James's head and started face smashing James so hard that, it was hitting the back of his throat, making him gag.

"Oh, daddy, I love this big black cock. Your wife don't give it to you like me, does she?" James asked, while stroking Lloyd's shaft. James begin sucking and stroking the shaft. James mouth was like a tight hole and before Lloyd knew it he busted off so hard in James's mouth—he swallowed every bit of it.

No one knew how much of a bitch James was. He was handsome and, masculine, and you would never know he sucked and took cock. Lloyd thought it was funny that when they went out, James had all the woman wanting him. He said he'd been with a few women but he preferred men.

"Get up and turn around," Lloyd ordered James, as he slid all ten inches deep and banged James to oblivion until they both came at the same time.

On his way home, Lloyd was angry with himself and his thirst for man goodies. James and Lloyd had both been virgins when they met. They both had the desire for men but never gave in to the feelings. Lloyd liked James a lot, but he would never let him know. Because Lloyd was not gay.

CHAPTER EIGHT

It was Thursday morning and Charlotte was thinking about James and their dinner tomorrow night.

Lloyd walked in the kitchen and said, "Oh, tomorrow I have to go to New Jersey."

Charlotte was irritated. "Lloyd, really?"

"Charlotte, don't start. If I don't work, you don't get to spend all the money you spend and sit at home."

"Lloyd, when will you make time for me," she asked angrily, slamming doors. "When, Lloyd?!" She stormed out of the kitchen.

Charlotte hoped that she had been convincing and felt that she performed very well for Lloyd to make him think she cared. But Charlotte was excited because now she would be able to spend time with James.

*****

As soon as Charlotte heard the door close and Lloyd pulling out the driveway to go to work, she called James to ask what time she should come for dinner on Friday.

"Oh, so you're going to let me cook for you?" he asked.

"Yes. What time is dinner?"

"At 8:00 pm, 'friend'," he said.

Charlotte giggled. "Ok, 'friend.' See you at 8!"

James hung up the phone and sat on the couch with his hands behind his head, thinking, *I love when a plan comes together. If I can't have Lloyd, I will help myself to his wife.* He laughed.

*****

Roger was on his way home when his phone rang. He looked down and it was a private number.

"Hello?" he said, but no one said anything. "Hello?"

Dial tone.

Roger made it home and Diane was in the kitchen cooking dinner.

"Hey Di," he said when he came in. "Where you at?"

"I'm in the kitchen!"

Roger walked up behind her and kissed her.

"Mmm, that smells delicious!"

"Go wash up," she said. "Dinner will be ready in ten minutes."

After dinner while Diane was washing the dishes, the phone rang and Diane ignored it. Roger yelled from the den, "Di, do you hear the phone?"

"Yes, someone has been calling all day for the last week or so. When I answer they wait for twenty to thirty seconds and then they hang up. I turned the phone off yesterday, but I get important calls on that phone.

"How long has this been going on?"

"It's been a week; I stopped answering."

"Well, if it continues, I will have the number traced."

Roger did not have a shadow of doubt that it was Tabatha.

*****

Charlotte arrived in front of James's apartment and James directed her to park in the rear so no one would notice her car. Getting out the car, Charlotte was nervous. She had never been to another man's place and thought to leave, but when she was turning around she saw James was in the lobby waiting to let her in.

"Hi, Charlotte. Come in, it's good to see you."

Charlotte, feeling out of place, said, "Hello, James."

"Don't worry, I don't bite." James put his hand on the small of Charlotte's back and led her into his apartment.

"It smells great. What are we having?"

"Chicken Alfredo. I hope you like it."

"Yes, I love pasta."

"Well then great, have a seat," he said as he pulled out Charlotte's chair.

James and Charlotte ate, talked, laughed, and enjoyed each other's company.

When they were finished eating, Charlotte said, "Thank you, dinner was great."

"Let me clean the table," James replied. "You can go make yourself comfortable."

Charlotte got up and headed into the living room. She was admiring the art James had on the walls and before she knew it he walked up behind her and put his hands around her waist. He started explaining each piece of art in detail. Charlotte was impressed and turned on at the same time. James didn't waste any time, since he realized how easy it was to get Charlotte to his place. He took her hand and led her to his bedroom. He lay Charlotte slowly on the bed.

"Do you want me to stop," he asked while gently kissing her lips, neck, chest, breasts, and stomach.

"Mmmmm, no, don't stop, please," she said.

James took his time and explored every part of Charlotte's body. They had sex all night until the next morning. Charlotte jumped up. She looked at her watch; it was 5:00 am. She hadn't meant to fall asleep!

"Oh shit," she said, grabbing her clothes with her heart beating out of her chest. "What in the hell was I thinking? I have to go—I know my husband is looking for me!"

"Calm down, everything will be all right."

"No, it won't," she said, rushing to get dressed. "I have to go."

Charlotte grabbed her cell phone from her purse and there were ten missed calls from Lloyd. She nervously tried to figure out what she was going to tell him.

When Charlotte got home, Lloyd's car was gone. She was glad; she needed to take a shower and figure out what to tell Lloyd. She called Lloyds phone, but there was no answer. She called the office, and he wasn't there. Where could Lloyd be? Charlotte undressed and got in the shower. Charlotte was fixing her ponytail and smiling, recounting her night.

"You must have had a fun night, smiling and all." Lloyd was standing in the doorway, clearly pissed off.

Charlotte turned around, startled and scared.

"Lloyd, hi. I didn't know you were home. I thought you were in New Jersey."

"Yes, I was. And then my meeting was canceled. Charlotte, where were you all night?"

"Oh my, Lloyd I tried calling you. Remember my college friend Maggie? She was in town and we went out to dinner and had drinks and—"

"Shut up, you lying bitch! I'm going to ask you again: where were you?"

"Lloyd, please. After dinner I wasn't feeling well so we went back to her hotel room and I fell asleep."

Lloyd backhand slapped Charlotte and she fell into the closet door. She tried to run and Lloyd caught her before she could go down the stairs. He was dragging her by her hair, but she managed to get loose.

Screaming and crying, she begged him to stop. Lloyd grabbed her by her hair again, threw her to the floor, and started kicking her.

"Lloyd, you're hurting me!"

"Shut up bitch," he yelled. "You are a lying, cheating whore!"

"Lloyd, please, I'm sorry," she begged through her tears.

Lloyd turned around and walked out of the room. He got in his car and dialed James's number.

*****

When James answered, Lloyd said, "Hey, I'm on my way over."

"Lloyd, wait, it's not a good time right now."

Lloyd was shocked to hear a man's voice in the background. "What do you mean it's not a good time right now? Oh I see, you have company, it's like that."

"Lloyd, it's only a family friend—"

Lloyd hung up before James could finish his sentence.

*****

Diane had just gotten out of the shower when she heard the doorbell.

"Coming!" she said. "Who is it?" she asked, looking through the peephole.

"This is the NYPD. Is Diane home?"

She unlocked the door. "Yes sir, I'm Diane."

"Hello ma'am. A few weeks ago you filed a report of vandalism to your house. We went to every house on this block and left our card with an anonymous number to report to if anyone had seen anything. We have someone who say they saw a woman."

"A woman?" Diane said, shocked.

"Do you or your husband have anyone you may know that may have an issue with you two, maybe an old jealous girlfriend or boyfriend?"

"You already asked us that, officer. NO, we don't."

"Well, ma'am, we will call you if we find the woman."

"Thank you, I appreciate all your help."

"You're welcome, ma'am. Have a nice day."

Diane shut the door and went to the phone to call Roger.

"Hi, Di."

"Hi, handsome. A police officer came by to tell me they may have found the person who vandalized our home."

"Great," Roger said. "What did he say?"

"He said it was a woman."

Roger started to get nervous. "A woman? Do they know who it was?"

"No, they have to investigate and possibly bring her in."

"I'm glad they're on the job."

"Roger."

"Yes, baby?"

"The officer asked again if she could have been an old girlfriend."

Roger giggled to hide his nervousness. "Baby, you know that can't be."

"That's what I told the officer."

"Di, I have to go. Don't forget we have the grand opening of the club tonight."

"Yes, and I will be ready. Go and get some work done—you're the only one working."

Roger burst out laughing. "You're right; see you later. I love you, Di."

"I know. I love you more."

"I know," he said.

Things were getting worse for Roger and he needed to figure out what to do. Diane could not find out about the affair he had with Tabatha.

*****

Lloyd drove over to James's apartment and sat outside for a few hours to see who James had in there. He couldn't understand why he cared. Lloyd said repeatedly to himself that he wasn't gay; he would never be seen with James except behind closed doors. *If that was the case*, he thought, *then why can't I get this man out my system?*

Lloyd tried calling James's phone several times, but there was no answer. Snapping out of it, Lloyd thought, *What is wrong with me? I need to go*. There was no sign of anyone, but the lights were on in James's apartment. As Lloyd was driving off he heard a few deep laughs and he saw James walking out with an older gentleman, who he'd never seen before. Lloyd sat there watching as they laughed, and the gentleman put his hand on James's shoulder, leaned forward, and kissed him.

What the fuck? thought Lloyd. *Oh, now I see this bitch mother fucker cheating! Wait, why do I care?* Lloyd turned on the lights and drove off fast, heading for the bar. James looked up and thought that he saw Lloyd's car but wasn't sure.

Lloyd got home furious and drunk and went straight to his study. Charlotte was sleep. Lloyd called James.

James's voice was half sleep and groggy when he answered after several rings.

Lloyd was silent for a moment, and then he said, his voice thick with drink, "Where you been tonight?"

"What do you want, Lloyd? Are you drunk?"

"What do I want? I want what's mine!"

"Look, Lloyd, I'm tired of the games. You tell me you're not gay and you want to end it, you're married, I barely see you and only on your terms. So guess what, Lloyd? I'm moving on."

"Now is not the time for the BS, James. You had no problem with our arrangement before. It's simple, let that dude know you can't see him anymore."

84

"An arrangement? That's what this was to you—an arrangement?! No, Lloyd, it's over. Stay with your wife. At first I was scared to leave because I love you. I know you don't love me, but I want to be loved and I'm ready to come out. I'm sick of lying to myself and others."

"James, look, let's talk about this," Lloyd said, lowering his voice.

"Talk about what? 'Us'? We have talked for years about 'us' and nothing has changed."

"Ok, ok, you got it, and I got you," Lloyd said, the anger coming back.

"Look, you're drunk. Let's talk face to face in a few days. Let me know your schedule and we can meet."

"Yes, let's do that. I will let you know later this week." Lloyd hung up.

James held the phone, laughing because his plan was coming together. The guy Lloyd saw him with that night was an old family friend with benefits, who James saw every once in a while when he needed some money. It wasn't by chance that James had run into Charlotte. He loved Lloyd, but enough was enough.

*****

85

Charlotte woke up well rested when her phone was ringing from a private number.

"Hey what's up," he said. "I haven't heard from you."

"Donte what do you want? There's been so much going on here with my husband," she answered.

"Where is he now?"

"At work—and no, Donte, you can't come over."

"I know you miss this. Your husband doesn't give it to you like I do. And I miss you."

"Donte, I have to go. Please, I will call you."

"Charlotte, I haven't seen you in weeks. I need you and you need me; we became close, and I know how you feel about me—"

Charlotte cut him off. "We have to stop this before someone gets hurt. I'm married and I'm sorry."

"You're sorry? He laughed, but there was anger in his voice. "We will stop when I say so! I know where you live. How would your husband feel if I told him I was sleeping with his wife for the last two years?"

"Donte, sweetheart, that isn't necessary. We said no feelings involved."

"No! Charlotte, you said that—I didn't. I fell in love with you."

"Take it easy; let's meet soon to talk."

"I want to see you tonight! I will be over at our usual time," he said and hung up.

"Wait, Donte! Not—" she started to say, but then she heard the dial tone.

Charlotte knew that Lloyd would be working late that night, and she also knew that she had been playing with fire when she started sleeping with Donte in her and Lloyd's home. She could not let Lloyd find out, and now on top of this she couldn't get James off her mind. Charlotte looked at the time; she knew Roger and Charlotte would be leaving soon for the grand opening at the club.

CHAPTER NINE

Diane was ready when Roger got home, just doing a few touch ups with her makeup. Roger walked over to kiss her on her forehead.

"Hey my queen, he said, running into the bathroom.

"Hey, are you ready?"

"Ready as I'm going to be. And damn, you look hot!"

"Yeah, so your groupies can see you have a wife."

Roger smiled. "They're definitely going to see. Can I get some before we go?"

"No," she said, fixing his tie, "but if you're good we can sneak off somewhere at the club tonight."

"Good, then I'm going to be on my best behavior, I love my special dark chocolate" he said, laughing.

Diane laughed too. "Come on, Mr. Nasty, let's go."

Roger followed her, still laughing. "You make me this way," he said, smacking Diane's butt.

Charlotte heard Roger and Diane's car and peeked out the window to watch them drive off. She was thinking, *This is too close. I can't continue to do this with Donte.*

*****

Roger and Diane pulled up to valet and got out of the car. Everyone who was everyone was at the club and they both looked grand. Lights, camera, and action—every step they had to stop to shake hands and greet people. A few people were shocked because many didn't know that Diane was African American. She didn't hang out much with her husband before with her busy schedule, but now that she hadn't written a book recently, she had more time to spend supporting him.

They got into the club and it was packed. They were escorted to the VIP area and it was lit. The bottles of Moet, Hennessey, and shots of Jack were flowing, and by 12:30 am they were good and drunk.

"Di, I will be back. I have to go to the bathroom," Roger said in her ear over the loud music of the club.

"Ok, baby."

Roger walked to the bathroom. It was down a long, semi-dark hallway, and when he turned the corner, Tabatha was standing in the dark corner. Roger was startled.

"Hi, Roger."

"Why in the hell are you following me?! What are doing here? I told you to stay away from me and my wife."

"Guess what, Roger? I'm here to tell your wife about us, but if I can see you tonight after the club, maybe we can work something out."

Roger grabbed Tabatha by the neck and shoved her into the dark corner, looking at her with clenched teeth.

"Mmm, baby, I remember you like it rough," she teased.

"Tonight is not the night. I will—"

"You will what, Roger?" she interrupted him with a smirk on her face. "See you tonight," she said as she walked away, glancing over her shoulder with a wink.

Roger headed back to his table looking a bit flushed in the face.

"You ok, baby?" Diane asked.

"Yes, the owner wants to meet after to go over our next move."

"That's great because I have an early meeting with my publicist in the morning. I'll get a cab home."

"Yes, Di, you go home and get some rest."

Roger and Diane walked toward the door to go out to hail her a cab, and Tabatha walked right up to them.

"You must be the lovely Mrs. Smith," she said to Diane. "I've heard so much about you."

Diane smiled. "Yes, I am. And you are…?"

"Tabatha," she said, extending her hand. "Roger and I did some business a long time ago, and I heard he would be here, and here I am."

"Well I've never heard of you, but thanks for coming and it was nice meeting you. Tabatha, right?"

"Yes, nice to meet you too. Are you leaving?"

"Yes, I have to leave this handsome man," she said, gently touching Roger's face and kissing him. "I have an early meeting."

"Well, again, nice to meet you—and don't worry, he's in good hands."

Diane was caught off guard, but she smiled as she looked Tabatha up and down. "I'm sure."

While waiting for a taxi, Diane said, "That was odd. Tabatha, is a nice looking young lady. What business did the two of you have?"

"She had a private party for her husband or boyfriend and we DJ'd it. Then she thought about opening a club herself but I'm not sure what happened," he lied.

A cab pulled up and Roger opened the door for Diane to get in. He kissed her and assured her he would be home as soon as the meeting was over.

"Be safe and text me when you get in," he said while kissing her through the window."

"Sure thing," she replied, still kissing him. "Be good—and hurry home if you want some."

"Mmm," he said, licking her bottom lip. "I will. See you later."

On the way home Diane couldn't stop thinking about Tabatha and how odd it was that she walked up knowing her name while Diane knew nothing about her. She felt sure she'd seen her before. She knew mostly all of Roger's business deals but she'd never heard of Tabatha.

*****

Charlotte heard a tap on the side door and opened it immediately, peeking out the door a bit nervously.

"What's wrong with you," Donte asked.

"Just making sure my neighbors aren't home. There's been some vandalism in our community and everyone is watching now."

"No one saw me," he assured her, pulling her to him. "But I'm glad to see you. I missed you." He kissed her neck.

Charlotte pulled away. "Donte, you said talk—let's talk."

"You know I don't want to talk. You know what I want," he replied, grabbing Charlotte aggressively.

"Donte, stop," she protested, trying to break loose from his strong hold. "Stop, please, let me go. You're hurting me!"

"Let you go," he said, getting pissed. "I've tried several time to let you go, but you kept and keep pursuing me." He punctuated that last word by hitting his chest.

"I know, and I'm sorry."

Donte walked toward the window and then turned around. "You know I fell in love with you, and I know you care for me. I've been sneaking around with you, making it convenient for you."

Charlotte moved toward him. "I know, and I'm sorry. I didn't mean to hurt you. Just calm down."

"Calm down?! Did you hear me? I love you!"

"Donte, you have to go please before my husband gets home."

Donte sat down. "I'm not leaving until I get what I came for, and I want it now. He grabbed Charlotte.

"Wait, Donte—let me go freshen up," she said, startled by his loud voice.

"No! Turn around," he said as he pushed Charlotte over the chair. He was already erect as he yanked Charlotte's robe up and roughly tore off her panties. He shoved his massive young penis deep inside her, grabbing her hair.

Charlotte started off fighting, but eventually gave in and started moaning and groaning.

"Yeah," he said. "Give it to me."

"Oh, it feels so good! I've missed this so much. Harder—harder!"

Donte went harder and harder, deeper and deeper, but just when Charlotte was about to cum Donte pulled it out.

"What are you doing? Why did you stop?" she panted.

Donte didn't say a word as he pulled up his pants and started out the door.

Charlotte followed behind him. "What's wrong? Where are you going? We're not finished!" she said, grabbing Donte by the arm.

"Yes, we are."

Charlotte slapped him, screaming at him to get out. "We are done! Don't call me, text me, or even look my way, asshole!" She slammed the door behind him.

*****

Diane got home, and as she stepped out of the taxi she saw someone leaving Charlotte's house, fixing his zipper. She was trying to make out who the person was and she realized it

94

was the same young guy she'd seen having sex with Charlotte before, that time when she was peeping through the window.

Oh my, she thought. That's the young guy from the grocery store. What is he doing leaving Charlotte's place this late at night?

Diane tried calling Roger, but there was no answer.

*****

The club let out and Roger went to Tabatha's place. As he was getting there, his phone started vibrating. It was Diane calling, so he let it go to voicemail. He got to Tabatha's door and rang the doorbell. Tabatha came to the door half dressed, as usual, opening the door and then walking away.

"Come in," she said, over her shoulder.

Roger was thinking, *Damn, look at that ass*, but snapped back to reality when the second call came from Diane.

"I'm sure that's your wife," Tabatha said.

Roger was sluggish and drunk, but anger flared in his eyes. "Yes, but keep her name out of your mouth and stay the hell away from her."

"Roger, you're not going to get rid of me that easily."

"We were never together, so I don't have to get rid of you. Just leave me and my wife alone."

Tabatha's voice rose with anger. "No, you got it wrong. You weren't saying that when your wife was on tour and you were all up in my shit. Hell, I thought you weren't married!"

Roger yelled back. "You knew I was married and you said no strings attached. We had fun for a moment, that's all."

"Fun, Roger! We had fun? No! We had a relationship—a relationship that lasted a year!"

"I was wrong. It shouldn't have happened. I love my wife."

Tabatha walked up to Roger and started unbuckling his pants.

Roger pushed her away. "No, I can't," he said, but he was so drunk the words come out slurred.

"Yes, you can," she said, groping and massaging his semi-erect penis through his pants.

"Tabatha, I'm married and I have to get home." His phone started vibrating.

"Your wife is calling again," Tabatha said as she pushed Roger down in the chair and proceeded to unbutton his pants. "Stop fighting. You could never resist my blowjobs, and if you want me to keep us a secret, I suggest you give me what I want. If not, I will tell your wife everything."

At this point Roger felt he had no way out. If letting Tabatha suck him off would keep her quiet, then so be it.

Roger took his erect penis out his pants and shoved it in Tabatha's mouth. She sucked his cock until he came in her mouth. With no words, Roger got up and left.

On the way home, Roger pulled the car over, stewing with anger that he had given in to Tabatha. *I have to pull it together*, he thought. If I lose Diane, my life will never be the same. She cannot find out about me and Tabatha. Roger tried to pull himself together as he pulled into the driveway. He was hoping Diane would be sleep, since she had been calling him all night and he hadn't answered. But when he opened the door he heard the TV on in the family room.

"Hey Di, you're up late."

"Yes," she said, clearly irritated. "I've been calling you and you didn't answer. I called the club and they said you had left over two hours ago."

"Di, you know how it is, we took our party to another club. Come here, give me a kiss."

"No, Roger. You're drunk and you never have not answered my calls before." She stared at him. "Roger, don't play with me."

"Di, what's wrong? What are you saying?"

"I'm not saying anything. Or is there something you want to say me?"

"Di, wait," he said, drunkenly stroking his cock. "I thought you wanted some."

"I'm going to bed. You can do yourself Roger, or maybe whoever you were with tonight." Diane stalked out the room.

"Di come here, come here baby." He got up to stop her.

"What, Roger, what?! We've been here before."

"Di, you know me. I wouldn't do anything to hurt—"

Diane put up her hand to stop him. "Don't, Roger. Please don't give me a reason not to trust you again."

Roger pulled Diane to him, holding her and rubbing her hair and back. She rested her head on his chest.

"Something don't feel right, Roger."

Roger grabbed her face. "Listen baby, you are my queen, you know I love you. You are my breath, my life." Diane began tearing up, and Roger was wiping her face. "Di, you don't have to worry. There's no one and nothing more important than you."

"I'm tired," she said. "I'm going to bed."

"Ok, I will be up shortly."

Diane's mind was racing. She also couldn't get what she saw tonight off her mind, the young guy from the grocery store leaving Charlotte's house. And she definitely didn't think it was a good idea to tell Roger.

Roger sat on the couch with his face in his hands, rubbing his throbbing head. He was thinking, *What have I done? I shouldn't have let Tabatha in again. I can't lose Di—I can't. What in the hell have I done?*

CHAPTER TEN

Lloyd called Charlotte and said he would be late, as always. She had nothing to do, so she decided to call James, but he didn't answer.

James was sitting across from Lloyd at the hotel bar when Charlotte was calling, and he pushed ignore.

Taking a sip of his drink, James asked, "So what was the excuse tonight?"

"I don't need an excuse," Lloyd answered. "I just said I would be late."

"So you got it like that?"

"Yeah, I got it like that," he said, throwing back shots of Jack. "Let's go to the room to talk."

"Nah, I want to enjoy some time out. Look at those ladies looking over here." James waved at them, and they waved back.

"What are you doing? Why do you do that? If you prefer men, why do you continue to mislead women?"

"I'm just having fun, man, that's all. You're married—seems to me you're misleading your woman. Anyway, why do you care what I do?"

Lloyd was starting to get loud. "Why do I care? This is my life we're talking about! I'm not trying to catch any diseases!"

"Whatever," James said, getting up as he took his last shot. "You said you wanted to break it off, so I will see you later. I'm going to the room."

Lloyd shook his head. He stood up several minutes later and followed James, making sure no one saw him. Lloyd used his key to get in, James was naked, getting in the shower.

"Join me if you want," he said to Lloyd.

"We need to talk," Lloyd repeated. But the liquor was kicking in, preventing him from controlling his thoughts. *Damn, he looks good and I miss that tight ass.* Lloyd stripped down and got in the shower behind James.

As always, James started sucking Lloyd's erect penis. Lloyd stood James up and started kissing him. *It has to be the liquor*, he thought. *I have never kissed James.* Kissing was too intimate and it made Lloyd feel gay. *I'm not gay*, he thought. But James was loving it. Lloyd turned James around and gave him every inch, thinking about Charlotte. Some time passed and it was getting late. The liquor was wearing off and Lloyd was disgusted remembering kissing James.

"What got into you tonight?" James asked him.

Lloyd was getting dressed. "What do you mean 'what got into me tonight?'"

We've been together for twenty years off and on, and you've never kissed me."

"I don't know. But you need to tell that other dude it's over. I have to go."

"When will I see you again? Lloyd, you can't run my life. You have a wife, and I've dealt with that for several years."

Lloyd was angered by James's response. "You knew what it was when we started, and you were fine with it. Like I said, tell that dude it's over."

"Whatever man, I will see you later."

Lloyd slapped James and grabbed him around his neck with one hand, choking him. James wasn't a fighter; he looked like he could do something but he's was so weak.

"I shouldn't have to ask twice," Lloyd told him.

James was startled. "What's gotten into you? Get off of me!"

"Like I said."

James was holding his neck where it hurt. Speaking loudly, he said, "I know, and I heard you."

"Let me find out that dude's been with you and you will definitely see a whole other side of me," Lloyd said as he walked out the door.

James was scared and turned on at the same time. He was thinking, Lloyd is my man and he loves me. Although he hasn't said it to me, his actions show he cares.

*****

Diane hadn't spoken to Charlotte, even after seeing what she saw the other night. She decided to call her.

"Hi, Diane."

"Hi, how are you and how have you been?"

"Great," Charlotte said, "and you?"

"I'm fine. An officer stopped by a few weeks ago to give me update, apparently someone called the anonymous line and reported that they saw a woman the night our house was vandalized. They're not sure who it was yet; they're still investigating and said they will call me when they find the woman."

"What—a woman?!"

"Yes, and then the officer had the nerve to ask if it could be an old jealous girlfriend or boyfriend."

"Well," Charlotte reassured her, "you don't have to worry; Roger isn't that type of guy."

"That's what I said. Anyway, what have you been up to?"

"Nothing. We have a lot to catch up on, though. When will you be free? Let's go out to dinner."

"Next week works for me," said Diane.

"How about next Wednesday?"

"That works for me."

"Good. It's a date—see you then!"

*****

As Charlotte hung up with Diane, another call was coming through, and it was James.

"Hi Charlotte, how are you?"

"I'm fine. What do you want? I haven't heard from you since we had dinner."

"...and..."

"'And' what? I don't remember anything but dinner," she said.

"Oh," said James, laughing. "That's all you remember? I remember your body and those moans."

Charlotte giggled. "It doesn't matter; I have to go."

"Charlotte, wait, I'm sorry. I've been busy and you have been on my mind. I want to see you again."

"James, I don't want things to get complicated. I enjoyed the other night."

"Me too. That's why I want to see you again, 'friend'."

Charlotte was silent for a moment, then said, "James, we shouldn't be doing this. I'm married."

"I know; you have told me so several times—yet you still ended up in my bed."

"James, it's hard for me to leave my house."

"Well, Charlotte, I can sneak over after hours when your husband is gone or out of town. When is the next time he'll be leaving?"

"I'm not sure but I will let you know."

"Soon please," James said. "I miss you."

"Bye, James," she said as she hung up the phone, smirking as she thought of the night she had spent with him and how much she was looking forward to seeing him again.

*****

It was almost 5:00. Lloyd was leaving the office and he needed to stop at the grocery store to get a few things. As he was walking around the store he noticed Donte and walked over to him.

"What's up, young man?" he asked.

"Hi, sir."

They shook hands.

"How have things been going? I see you're still here."

"Yeah, things have been going fine, but I've been looking for another job and nothing has come through."

"I recall you said you took a few business courses in college, right?"

"Yes, sir."

"Well here's my card, Call my Assistant Liz on Monday and we can see if we have any job openings."

The excitement was obvious in Donte's voice. "Thank you, sir, will do!"

When Lloyd got home, he could smell dinner cooking.

Charlotte said, "Hey Hun, go freshen up for dinner."

"Hi," Lloyd said, walking into the kitchen, distracted. "What's for dinner?"

"Spaghetti. Is everything ok?"

"I'm fine. It's been a long day, and I'm tired."

"Well, let's sit down and eat," she said, sitting down.

"I stopped at the grocery store to pick up a few things and ran in Donte."

106

Charlotte was puzzled and looked away to hide it. "Donte?"

"You know, the young guy who works at the grocery store."

"Oh yeah," Charlotte said.

"I gave him my card to call the office Monday. He has a degree in business and he's been looking for a job but he hasn't landed anything yet."

Charlotte hid her emotions. "That's great you're helping the young black man."

"Yes, I try; he's a hardworking young man."

"Well, what do you have planned this weekend?"

"Not much. I have a late meeting Friday night. What about you?"

"My friend Maggie will be in town. She called and wanted me to go to dinner, but I wanted to make sure you were ok with it."

"I'm ok with it. Why wouldn't I be?" he said, looking up from his dinner.

"We both know, Lloyd. I can't do much without it being a problem."

"Go out and enjoy yourself," he said, getting up from the table. "I'm going to my study to do some work."

"Ok, I'm going to clean up. Oh, I almost forgot, I spoke to Diane and the police said they have an eyewitness who said they saw a woman leaving their house.

Lloyd stopped in his tracks. "A woman?"

"Yes, a woman."

"Well, I hope they find her. But why would a woman do that?"

Charlotte shrugged. "That's what both Diane and I said. Either way, they are trying to close the case soon."

"Good, keep me posted," he said, walking out.

Charlotte watched Lloyd walk out of the kitchen. As soon as she heard his study door close, Charlotte grabbed her phone to text James.

"What time do you want to meet?" she texted.

"You managed to find a way to get away! I should consider myself special," he texted back right away.

"Maybe you should," she shot back.

"Same time, 8:00 pm. I think we should meet across town at the Madison Hotel."

"Ok, see you then," she said.

Charlotte was in the best mood the rest of the night. She looked forward to getting out. Nothing could make her mad or get in her way right now—not even Lloyd. She managed to avoid him and their arguments all week.

CHAPTER ELEVEN

Roger knew he needed to come up with a plan to get rid of Tabatha. He couldn't continue to be blackmailed, so he called her.

"Hello," Tabatha said. "You must be calling to see me."

"No I'm not. Actually, I'm calling to let you know, no more private meetings for us. And for the record, if you want to tell my wife, go ahead. I don't care anymore."

"Roger, really?"

"Yes, really. Leave me and my wife alone. This is the last and final warning; don't call or text me anymore."

Tabatha laughed. "I'm sure you don't want me to tell your wife."

"You can tell her—I'm done!" Roger said and then hung up the phone.

He was nervous, but at this point he also didn't care anymore. He figured he would deal with it as it came along. He thought about how much he loved Di and how he'd made a terrible mistake that could cost him his marriage. Roger called Di.

"Hi, handsome," she answered.

"Hi, gorgeous, what are you up to?"

"I'm cooking dinner and about to throw some clothes in the washer. What's up?"

"Nothing. Can we talk tonight at dinner"?"

"Sure, baby—everything ok?"

"Yes, I just have a few things I want to discuss with you."

"Ok, then please pick up a bottle of wine. This seems serious."

Roger giggled. "Ok, see you later."

Diane hung up feeling a bit uneasy. The last time Roger had called to let her know they needed to talk it wasn't good. She wondered, What now?

Diane was loading the washer going, through Roger's pants pockets for trash and she found a crumpled parking ticket. She checked the date, time, and location; it was late, and it was from the night of the club's grand opening. *That's odd*, she thought, because he has free parking around the clubs and bars that he frequents. There was a knock at the door. Diane put the ticket in her pocket and ran to the door to open it.

"Hi, Officer. How may I help you?"

"Hi, Mrs. Smith. I have some good news: the anonymous caller's information panned out, and we have the anonymous caller coming in to the precinct next week to see if she can identify the woman who vandalized your home. We thought you would like to be a part of it."

"Yes sir. What day and what time?"

"Monday at 9:00 am."

"Ok, sir, I will be there."

Diane hung up happy to hear the good news that the woman who did this was going to have charges brought against her. She heard the front door open and Roger come in.

"Di, I'm home," he said.

"I'm in the den," she said. "Come in here."

"Hey, what's up?"

"The police officer stopped by a few minutes ago and said that the anonymous caller's info panned out and they have the caller coming in to the precinct next week to see if she can identify the woman who vandalized our home. They let me know because they thought I would like to be a part of it."

"That's great! Are you going?"

"Yes, definitely! And I'm going to bring charges against her."

"Right," he agreed. "Do you need me to go with you?"

"If you're not busy, that would be great."

"Good, I'm going."

Diane kissed him. "Thank you, baby!"

"Let me go change and I will be down in a minute for dinner. Roger returned immediately and they sat down to enjoy their dinner.

As they were finishing, Roger said, "Dinner was great."

"What did you want to talk about?" Diane asked him.

"It's been a long day; it can wait."

"Ok, I'm going to take a shower."

Diane know Roger so well that she knew he had something to tell her. She wasn't sure what, but she would get to bottom of this. When Roger fell asleep Diane decided to google the address on the ticket. It was an apartment complex downtown, and Diane made a mental note to drive by it very soon.

*****

Charlotte was getting dressed when Lloyd came in.

"You look nice," he said.

Charlotte was shocked; he hasn't said that in a while. "Thank you," she said.

"Where are you girls going?"

"Not sure, maybe downtown."

"Ok," he said. "I'll be working; see you later."

Charlotte was surprised how easy it was tonight with Lloyd, which made her wonder what he was up to. But she didn't really care as long as she was going out without a fight.

She arrived at the hotel at ten minutes to 8:00. When James arrived they chatted a little, laughed, and played truth or dare. James shared his life story and Charlotte shared part of her story, or the good parts at least.

Charlotte couldn't share with James that she was brought up in a trailer park in Oklahoma. Her dad was a construction worker and an abusive alcoholic, and her mother was a waitress in the small community diner. Charlotte would always dream about a fancier life. They barely had food, they had more bills than money, and when Charlotte turned sixteen she set out to be an actor. Charlotte fell into the wrong hands and started stripping, which lead her to become a high-class hooker. Things got so bad for Charlotte she had to leave Oklahoma to New York, where she started a new life.

"So your husband is barely home?"

"He works a lot or he's out of town."

"How do you ladies put up with our schedules?"

"Lloyd is the provider; I don't work."

"What did you do before Lloyd?"

"I was a secretary. Actually, I was Lloyd's secretary. When he asked me to marry him, I quit the firm."

"Wow, interesting."

"What about you? What do you do?"

"I'm a consultant for small firms."

"What kind of consultant?" she asked.

"Financial."

"That sounds interesting."

"It is," he said. "But enough of me, I want to explore you."

"Explore me," Charlotte asked. "What do you mean?"

James guided her to the bed. "Let me show you, he said, as he laid her on her back. He started from her head, removing everything down to her feet with tender kisses and gentle touches over her breasts, navel, and thighs. "How does this feel?"

"Good, so good," Charlotte answered, her eyes closed, enjoying every moment.

James's phone started vibrating. He reached for it and immediately rejected the call. It was Lloyd.

"Who was that?" Charlotte asked.

"Don't worry, it's my sister. I will call her back later."

"Good, please continue."

"Sure," he said. "My pleasure."

James spread Charlotte's legs wide open and buried his face between her legs. Charlotte had a thing for black men; she couldn't control it. James came up for air and started kissing

Charlotte. She put James on his back, straddled him, and rode his penis like a savage beast until he came all over himself.

James massaged his still erect penis. "Damn, that was good. Where did that come from?"

Charlotte replied, "There's a lot where that came from."

"Well, I'm looking forward to it," he responded.

Charlotte kissed James and said, "I have to get ready to go."

"Why so soon?" he protested. "Please stay a little while longer!"

"I can't," she said. "Lloyd is home tonight and I don't want to raise any red flags. We have to be careful."

"You're right. It's just I enjoy spending time with you."

"Well that's good, were going to be spending a lot of time together," she said, smiling.

"I haven't felt like this in a long time and I don't want you to go.

Charlotte finished putting on her clothes and fixing her hair. "I know and I'm sorry, I have to go. I will walk myself out, thank you."

"Thank me for what?"

"A wonderful evening and sharing a part of yourself with me. It's been a long time since I've connected with another man."

"Well this is the beginning of a new friendship," James said.

"Yes," Charlotte agreed. "A new friendship. See you soon."

James- stood at the door, gazing at Charlotte. "You sure you have to go?"

"Yes."

"Ok, then I'll see you soon."

James shut the door and couldn't help but daydream about Charlotte. He seemed to be falling for her and didn't understand his feelings.

CHAPTER TWELVE

Diane was up early Saturday morning heading to her meeting with the publicist. The meeting went well, and on her way home she recalled that the apartment complex from the ticket in Roger's pocket was near. She put it in her GPS and headed that way.

The apartment complex looked nice, but Roger had told her they left the club that night and went to a local bar to meet. Roger knew that Diane would trust him until he gave her a reason to doubt him, and her gut told me something wasn't right.

Diane went home and went straight to her office to get on the computer. She thought of the night of the grand opening and the odd meeting with the young lady, Tabatha. She decided to google Tabatha. She wasn't sure if it was the right Tabatha, since the address on file was old and from another state. And this girl had been arrested for disorderly conduct, stalking, vandalism. Diane thought, *Vandalism*?

*****

The weekend went by really quickly, and Roger and Diane were on their way to the precinct. Roger hadn't talk to Tabatha since he told her it was over and she could tell his wife if she wanted. They got to the precinct, and after an hour, the anonymous caller behind the glass had come up with nothing. Diane noticed that Roger was on edge the whole time at the precinct but she ignored it because she was going to do her own investigation. When Diane got home she called in a favor to a close friend, Dexter, who could get any information you needed that you couldn't get otherwise.

"Hello Dexter, it's Diane."

"Diane," he said, clearly excited to hear from her. "How are you? Long time no hear!"

"I'm fine, Dexter. I called because I need a favor. Roger is hiring again. Can you pull a young lady for me? I just need to know her last name, current address, where she worked previously and works currently, etc."

"Anything for you Diane, no problem. Send me her name and info, and give me until end of the week."

"Sure Dexter—and please don't mention this to Roger."

"No problem, I will get back to you at the end of the week."

"Thank you," Diane said. "I appreciate it."

*****

Charlotte and Diane decided to eat out at Simply Delish.

"I'm so glad we came out," Charlotte told her over drinks. "I needed a break."

"Me too," Diane said, clearly bothered by something.

Charlotte took a bite of her food. "Are you ok? You don't seem yourself."

"I'm fine," Diane said. "There's so much going on with my writing, that's all."

"Well I can help you, girl—my life is full of drama!"

They both laughed.

Diane told her, "We went down to the precinct Monday and the anonymous caller couldn't make a positive ID."

"I know that must have pissed you off."

"Yes, it did, but I'm staying positive. Enough about me—what have you been up to?"

"Not much...Diane we been good friends for a long time. I can always count on you, and you have always been honest with me."

"Yes, of course. What's going on?" Diane showed her concern but already knew what Charlotte was going to tell her.

"Things aren't what they seem. I had an affair."

119

Diane calmly continued eating. "Really? But actually, I knew."

Charlotte was shocked. "Excuse me?"

"With the young guy Donte from the grocery store, right?"

Charlotte got quiet, feeling ashamed. She looked at Diane, "How did you know?"

"I knew when it started a year or two ago. I saw Donte several times leaving your house late at night when Lloyd was out of town. Also, one night I saw all the lights off except for the one in the den and I was wondering why the one light was on. I came over to check that everything was all right. I looked through the window and saw you two having sex."

Charlotte dropped her fork in total shock. "I love Lloyd," she explained, "but we don't spend time together, we don't have sex, and he has a terrible temper! He hits me sometimes."

Now it was Diane's turn to be surprised. "Hit you? No, not Lloyd."

"Yes, Diane, Lloyd is physically abusive. He calls me a liar and a cheat! That's why you don't see me for weeks, I have to wear a lot of makeup and dark shades to heal."

"Oh Charlotte, I'm sorry," she said, touching her hand. "Does he know about Donte?"

"No, I broke it off with Donte. Then Lloyd ran into Donte a few weeks ago and offered him a job with the company."

"Charlotte, what are you going to do if Lloyd finds out?"

"I'm hoping he doesn't and Donte moves on."

"Charlotte, Lloyd shouldn't be putting his hands on you. You understand that, right? But I'm glad you broke it off with Donte. And don't worry, I didn't mention it to Roger because he said to mind my business."

"Diane, you're a great friend."

"Yeah, yeah, yeah—but I don't like what's going on. Just be careful. At this point with so much going on I can't be in other folks' business, so just be careful."

"I will. I'm so glad I finally said something, it was bothering me."

Diane- put her finger up to say "Give me a minute" as her phone rang.

"Hello?

"Diane hey," Dexter said. "I have some information for you."

"I wasn't expecting to hear from you until Friday."

"Well I had some time on my hands and figured I would get it done. You'll be surprised. Can you meet me at my office tomorrow morning?"

"Yes. What time is good for you?"

"How about 10:00 am?"

"Ok, see you then," Diane said and hung up.

"Who was that?" Charlotte asked, sipping her wine.

"My publicist," Diane lied. "She wants to go over a few things tomorrow."

"Good! Hurry up and get that book done, so I can purchase a few for my nieces."

"Thank you. I appreciate your support."

"You know I wouldn't have it any other way

Diane sat back, staring at Charlotte while smiling and shaking her head.

Charlotte smiled back. "What, Diane?"

"Nothing. I'm just glad you finally told me; I was waiting."

Charlotte laughed. "Whatever! I was going to bust; that's why I suggested dinner."

"Well, I enjoyed dinner. Let me pay this bill so we can get out of here."

"No, I invited you—it's on me."

"No problem," Diane said, handing over the check. "I'm not going to fight to pay."

They both burst out laughing

On the ride home Diane thought how nice it was to laugh with so much going on. But she also couldn't help but wonder what Dexter had that was interesting. When Diane got home, Roger was in the family room sleep. He heard her come in and stretched, slowly waking up.

"Hey, how was dinner," he asked.

"Hi baby, dinner was nice."

"Good," he said. "Come here." Diane walked over to Roger, and he sat her down on his lap. "I was up waiting for you."

Diane blushed. "For what?" Roger started kissing her seductively. "Mmm."

"Mmmhmm...you feel it? The one eyed monster missed you."

Diane reached for his groin. "Mmm, he's nice and ready."

"Always for you." Diane turned around to straddle Roger as he gently caressed her swollen breast and sucking her erect brown nipples.

"Oh, baby," she said, holding his head to her chest. "This feels so good," she moaned as she slowly rode his erect penis.

"Damn, I love this good-good."

"And I love Mr. Bigs," she said, seductively.

"Ohh shit, you know I can't last when you talk dirty to me."

"I know; you love this, don't you?"

"Yes," he said, getting over-aroused. Diane got up off his erect penis and put his whole manhood in her mouth. "Ohh damn," he said, grabbing Diane's head. She knew how to make Roger go crazy, so she started gagging and slurping, while she gently stroked his shaft, making it wetter and wetter. He went out of control. "What the hell, get up," he said, putting her on her back. "I want to taste you." Roger was looking in her eyes and she knew he loved her. He spread her legs wide and buried his face between Diane's legs, nibbling, licking, and sucking gently on her jewel. She loved the way Roger gave her head. Roger enjoyed it more than she did.

"Aww baby," she said, looking down at Roger. "I'm about to cum!"

"Cum, baby. Damn, Di, I love you so much. I love drinking your juices."

Diane grabbed Roger's head, slowly pushing his face and tongue deeper and deeper in her good-good.

"Di, you taste so good."

"I'm cumming baby! Don't stop! This shit feels so good. Awwwww, suck it baby gently, ohhh shittttt!!"

Now I want to feel it, said Roger

With her legs still wide open, Roger pulled Diane to the edge of the bed and slowly inserted his erect penis. He seductively and slowly kissed Diane, going deeper and deeper, working her walls, as if he was doing push up in it.

"Mmmmmm, Mmmmmmm, go deeper baby!" she begged.

Roger started going deeper and deeper, slowly stroking Diane's good-good.

"I'm about to cum! I love you so much!"

"Cum baby," she told him. "Cum inside me—I'm about to cum again, damnnnnn," she screamed, holding Roger tight.

Roger and Diane came together, moaning and groaning. Roger fell over panting on her chest, and Diane started rubbing Roger's head.

"I love you, baby," she said.

"I love you more," he said back, kissing Diane. "You are the best thing that ever happened to me."

"Ditto," she said, smiling and holding Roger's face to kiss him. "I know. Let's go to bed."

"I will be up in a minute," he said.

"Ok, don't be long."

Roger was stuck. He didn't know what had gotten into Di. That's what had turned him on to Diane when he met her: how smart she was, her sex drive, her beauty, and booty, he thought, smiling. I fell in love with her and she is everything to me; I don't know what I would do without her.

Diane got in the shower, smirking and thinking about how much she loved Roger. She thought, Roger is the love my life. I just want my husband to know all he needs is me and what he would be missing without me. He's mine—I will fight for what's mine.

*****

Roger left early the next morning for the office and texted Diane to tell her he would be late that night. He got to work early, and he had several missed calls on his phone from Tabatha. At noon after his meeting he walked into his office and Tabatha was sitting there.

Roger was startled. He looked around and quickly closed the door. "What are you doing here? Get the hell out! My wife drops in on me."

"Who cares?" she said, walking around his office and touching things. "That's how you treat your girlfriend?"

Roger laughed. "Girlfriend? You mean whore."

"Oh so you had sex with this whore for one year? Roger, that's a relationship."

"Look, Tabatha: we will never be anything. I love my wife and I would do anything—I mean anything—to keep you from her."

Tabatha got up, laughing. "Well, I will see you tonight."

"No, you won't. Bye, Tabatha" he said, not looking her way. "Shut the door behind you."

"Oh, and Roger, I think I'm pregnant."

Roger stood up. "What does that have to do with me? I haven't fucked you in a year, and the last time I saw you, you hit me off with some top piece.

"Roger, you were too drunk to remember."

"Remember what?!"

"We had sex. You were all over me, telling me how much you love me."

Roger jumped up and locked the door. He angrily grabbed Tabatha by the arm. "You stupid psycho lying bitch. I didn't fuck you that night! I will kill you!"

Tabatha actually showed fear for the first time. "Roger, you're hurting me!"

Roger let her go because of the knock on his office door. It was his assistant, Misty. "Hey, boss. Everything all right?"

"Yes, thank you."

"Let me go," Tabatha said, grabbing her purse and coat and walking out.

Misty looked at both of them, puzzled. "Boss, you sure you're ok? Who is that?"

"Yes I'm ok," Roger assured her. "That's an old acquaintance. Please shut the door behind you."

"Ok," Misty said and walked out the office.

*****

Diane got to Dexter's office ten minutes early.

Dexter came around from behind the desk to greet Diane with a hug. "Hello, stranger. You look great!"

"Hi, Dexter. Thank you! How is the family?"

"Everyone is fine, and yours?"

"Good, thank you—so what do you have?" she asked, settling in the chair.

"Well, her name is Tabatha McCarthy. She's a stripper and she works at The Doll House."

Diane looked puzzled. "A stripper? Isn't The Doll House on the other side of town?"

"Yes—and get this—she was arrested a few years ago for disorderly conduct, stalking, and vandalism. She was charged and put on probation. This girl isn't a good fit to hire," he advised, handing Diane the report.

Diane was shocked as she looked over the papers. "Mmmhmm, and where does she live?"

"Her address was hard to find so I called my friend at the precinct. Apparently, she's sub-leasing an apartment at The Alps downtown."

Diane's heart dropped and started beating harder. That was the apartment complex on the ticket she had found in Roger's pocket. *What connection does Roger have with this woman?* she thought. *I will soon find out.*

"Thank you, Dexter, this helped," she said, getting up to leave.

"Anytime, Diane."

Diane walked out angry and upset. She knew something wasn't right and it was time she got to the bottom of it. There was something up with Tabatha and Roger and she would find out what it was.

*****

Roger was leaving work and heading home when he received a text from Tabatha: "See you shortly."

"No," he texted back. "I'm in a late meeting. Don't text me."

"Your wife is on my speed dial."

"Call her. I'm tired of running. I'm not going to let you blackmail me any longer."

"Ok, ok, I'm sorry. Can we meet?"

"No," he texted back. "Leave me alone."

"Please, Roger, I'm sorry. Please, I need you."

"Leave me the hell alone, you crazy bitch."

Tabatha didn't like being called crazy. It set something off in her, and she decided it was time to make Roger pay for using her.

CHAPTER THIRTEEN

Lloyd hadn't seen James in weeks and decided to drop by his place. When Lloyd was walking up to the door he heard music and knocked.

James was shocked when he opened the door. "Lloyd, what are you doing here?"

"I was driving by and decided to stop in. I can stop by, can't I?"

"Lloyd, I'm busy," James said, with the door barely open. "I have company."

Lloyd was starting to get pissed. "So what are you saying?"

"You have to go. My sister is here. I will call you, but please don't make a scene."

"Ok, it's like that? I won't make a scene. Let me holla at you downstairs."

"Why downstairs?" James asked.

"I want to talk," Lloyd said, "but not around your company."

James grabbed his keys and motioned to whoever was there that he would be back. "I'm walking my friend downstairs; be right back."

They got down to Lloyd's truck and got in.

"What do you want to talk about?" James asked.

Lloyd was still pissed. "Where have you been? I haven't heard from you."

"Lloyd, you're not available for me."

"What are you talking about?"

"I need more, Lloyd, not what you're giving me."

"I will give you more time," Lloyd said, shaking his head. "Get rid of that dude. I mean it."

"You can't keep doing me this way. I love you."

Lloyd started stroking his penis. "Look, he misses you."

"I've got company, Lloyd, I have to get back upstairs."

"Yeah, you can go back up loaded with cum in your mouth."

"Fuck you, Lloyd," James said, grabbing for the door to get out.

"That's what you want. Tell that dude to go and I will give it to you. Come over here and put your mouth on it," he said, pulling James to him.

"No, Lloyd, this isn't right."

"So you don't want this monster? Ok, since you have to go, give me one of those sloppy sucks."

"Lloyd, please go. I'm done with you and us." James opened the car door to get out.

"James, I own you and I'm tired of playing games. Don't make me act a fool upstairs."

"No, please, Lloyd," James begged.

"Well then make me feel good," Lloyd responded, taking his erect penis out.

James really couldn't resist—he could never resist Lloyd or Lloyd's penis. It was so big and tempting. Lloyd laid his seat back and James leaned over and started slowly sucking Lloyd's cock until he came in his mouth. Lloyd buttoned up his pants.

"Wipe you mouth," he said. "That shit look nasty."

"Really, Lloyd?" James said, feeling used. "Fuck you." He got out of the car and slammed the door.

Lloyd yelled through the open window, "You want me to come up, tell that dude he has to go!"

"Go to hell!" James yelled back.

Lloyd drove off.

James got back upstairs, thinking, *Damn, that was close.*

Charlotte came out the back room. "Who was that?"

133

"The neighbor downstairs said we were making too much noise," James told her.

Charlotte giggled and whispered. "Really? Oh my, was I too loud?"

James laughed. "Yes, you were!"

Charlotte kissed James. "I have to go and get home before Lloyd."

"Call me to let me know you made it home."

"Ok, see you."

*****

Charlotte pulled into the driveway and was stunned to see Donte's car. *What the hell is going on?* she thought, nervous and scared as she walked into the house.

"Charlotte, we're in the den!" Lloyd called when he heard her walk in.

"Ok, let me freshen up and I will be in there in a minute."

"Ok!"

Lloyd turned back to Donte. "I want to introduce you to my wife."

Charlotte walked into the den and all she could think about was the many times she and Donte had sex in that room. Smiling, she went over to kiss Lloyd.

"Hi, honey."

"Charlotte, I want you to meet Donte. You know, Donte from the grocery store. I called him over to offer him the finance manager position."

"Yes, I remember Donte. Congratulations!" she said, reaching to shake his hand.

"Thank you Mrs. Web. You have a beautiful home."

"Thank you!"

Charlotte was shocked when Donte called her Mrs. Web. He'd acted as if he didn't know her! But when Lloyd turned his back to get a drink, Donte rubbed his groin, and Charlotte started shifting in her seat. She hadn't seen Donte much lately, and he was looking good.

"Honey," Charlotte said, "I think I'm going to go put something on to eat. It was nice to meet you, Donte."

"Nice to meet you too, Mrs. Web," he said, looking at Charlotte as if he could eat her alive.

Lloyd got a phone call and went into his study to take it. Covering the phone, he told Donte, "Give me fifteen or twenty minutes."

"No problem, sir." Donte gave himself his own tour of the house, and when he turned the corner, Charlotte was in the pantry. He pushed Charlotte's back against the pantry wall.

"Donte, what are you doing?" Charlotte whispered, scared. "My husband is in the other room, please move!"

"No, he took a call and went into his study. He said he would be fifteen or twenty minutes—all I need is five minutes."

"Donte, this is too close, please!" she said, pushing Donte away.

"He's still talking," Donte said, ignoring her. "I hear him. Turn around—hurry up!"

"Donte, this isn't right," she said, nervously.

But Charlotte couldn't resist. She lifted up her dress, and she wasn't wearing any panties. She bent over and Donte gave her several long and hard strokes. He came so hard and hurried to the bathroom to clean up. Charlotte was coming out of the pantry when Lloyd hit the corner.

"Where's Donte?" he asked, looking around.

Looking away nervous Charlotte replied, "I think in the bathroom; he asked to use the bathroom."

"Ok. Is dinner ready?"

"Yes, can you set the table?"

Lloyd set the table and they all sat down to dinner together.

After they were done, Donte said, "Well sir, I guess I will go. Everything was delicious; thank you, Mrs. Web."

"Anytime, Donte, you're part of the Web family now."

"Yes, Donte," Lloyd said, shaking his hand. "Welcome aboard."

Lloyd walked Donte to the door and watched him pull out of the driveway.

"That's a fine young man," he said to Charlotte. "He's going to be a good fit at WIF. I plan to take him under my wing."

"Yes he is; you made the right choice," she agreed as she was finishing up the dishes.

Lloyd walked up behind Charlotte, rubbing her shoulders, touching her hair. He turned her around, standing in front of her.

Kissing her, he said, "Dinner was great. And it turned me on the way Donte was looking at you."

"Lloyd," she said, annoyed. "What you are talking about?"

"I saw the way that young cat was looking at you," he said seductively.

"I didn't see it," she answered.

Lloyd pushed Charlotte against the counter and pulled one leg up. Putting his hand between her legs, "Mmmmm, no panties on."

"Oh Lloyd, don't stop! It feels so good!", with flashes of Donte on her mind

Lloyd put all ten inches inside Charlotte, and she cried out for more. "Harder, Lloyd!"

Lloyd pounded harder and harder, grabbing Charlotte's hair, biting her neck. You want it harder, said Lloyd

Yes, harder!" "Oh, oh, oh! I'm about to cum!

"Cum all over this cock! Yes, I'm about to cum too!"

"Cum, baby, give it to me!"

"Ohhhhhh, mmmmmmm, damn, damn, damn," he yelled. "I'm still cumming—ohhh shit, that was good!"

"Yes, baby. What got into you?"

"You. I haven't been treating you right," he said.

Charlotte was shocked by what Lloyd was saying. He hadn't been this open in months. She wasn't sure how long this would last. But it felt good that he was paying her some mind.

CHAPTER FOURTEEN

Roger called to say he had a late meeting, so Diane took it upon herself to ride by The Doll House to see if she could see any sign of Tabatha. She wasn't going to approach her; she just needed to see what's going on. Diane waited until it got dark so she wouldn't be noticed. She waited outside the place for several hours, and by 10:00 pm she saw Tabatha pull in. She was alone, pulling her luggage, and Diane watched her until she went in, then left.

When Diane got home she decided to look at the time of the ticket again. It was 4:00 am, the night of the grand opening at the club. *Why would this ticket be in his pocket?* she was thinking when her phone rang.

"Hello?" she said, but no one answered. "Hello? Hello?"

A raspy voice said, "You stupid bitch."

"Who is this?" Diane asked.

There was the sound of breathing on the line and then whoever it was hung up. Diane looked at the number, and it was blocked. The same person called back several times and hung up. Diane was angry and the next time they called she decided to let them have it.

"Hello! Stop calling this damn phone before I call the police!" she screamed.

"Di, what's going on?!" Roger asked, coming into the room.

"Sorry," she said. "Someone keeps calling this phone and hanging up. First they called me a stupid bitch."

"Really, Di? I'm going to get the number traced; this is getting out of hand."

"Yes, it is. I've had enough."

Roger knew that Tabatha was behind this. He needed to do something about her very soon.

*****

Several weeks had passed, and things only got worse. Roger and Diane's tires were slit, and the previous week someone had left a note that said, "You're going to pay bitch."

Roger had enough and finally called Tabatha. "Hey, we need to talk."

"Talk about what?" she asked. "You leaving your wife?"

"Look, enough of the games."

"What games, Roger? You used me and you know it. We didn't just have sex one time, we had sex a lot for a year. I don't think your wife would feel it was nothing."

"Tabatha, I'm sorry. I was lonely and I had no business treating you that way. I thought we had an understanding."

"We had fun, Roger. We are good together."

"No, we aren't. I could never be with you, Tabatha."

"You're hurting my feelings, Roger."

"I don't give damn about your feelings!"

Tabatha hung up and decided to drive by Roger's house. Diane was in the garage when she looked up and recognized Tabatha's car from the club the other night. Diane thought, *What in the hell is she doing in our neighborhood?* It was time Diane paid Tabatha a visit.

*****

Diane waited outside of the club for Tabatha to pull up. She remembered that she had come in at 10:00 pm last time. When she saw her car pull in, Diane hopped out her car.

"Excuse me, Tabatha?"

"Yes. You are…?"

"Diane, Roger's wife."You met me at the grand opening?

"Oh yes, what can I do for you?"

"You can stay away from my house and my husband."

Tabatha laughed as she walked into the building. "Whatever. What did your husband tell you?"

"Actually, he didn't tell me anything about you. I'm here on my own to warn you myself to stay away from my house and my husband."

Tabatha kept laughing and kept walking. "Tell Roger hi for me."

"Tabatha," Diane said.

"Yes?"

"Watch your back, sweetie. Consider yourself warned. I'm sure you don't know who you're messing with."

Tabatha went into the building, scared and nervous, thinking, *His damn wife is crazy! How did she find me and my information?* Tabatha tried calling Roger, but her calls went straight to voicemail.

*****

Charlotte hadn't seen much of Donte since he'd started at the firm. But finally she started seeing more of him because of the many company parties, including this year's promotion party, that were held at the Webs' house.

She noticed Donte across the room talking to Roger's assistant, Misty. Misty was young and beautiful; she had a lot going for herself and Charlotte was feeling kind of jealous. Although she'd been seeing James, she also missed Donte and the way he did this certain thing with his tongue done there. She started getting hot and bothered thinking about it, but was interrupted by Lloyd.

Lloyd kissed her forehead. "Everything ok?"

"Yes, do you need anything?"

"No, only you," he replied.

Charlotte looked at Lloyd with surprise, thinking, *Where is all this coming from?* "Good," she answered. "I'm all you need."

Lloyd walked off, and Donte walked over.

"Hi, Mrs. Web."

"Hello, Donte. Why so formal?"

"I think it's best we do it that way. I work for your husband now, and things have changed."

"So what," she said, smiling and looking around. "All we have to do is be careful, right?"

"I've been spending a lot of time with Liz."

Charlotte was shocked and pissed, but just placidly kept sipping her wine. "Liz? What can she do for you?"

"I can be with her when I want to since she doesn't have a husband."

"Oh, now it's a problem," she said, the jealousy apparent in her tone.

Lloyd noticed Charlotte and Donte's body language and walked over to them.

"Is everything ok with you two?" he asked.

"Yeah, Donte was just saying how much he enjoys his position."

"Yes sir, and I had to let Mrs. Web know how good the food is tonight."

"Yes, she's a great cook," Lloyd said. "Come with me so I can introduce you to our regional manager."

Donte and Lloyd walked off, and Charlotte steamed at the fact that Donte is dating Liz. Her phone rang. It was James, so she went out on the patio to talk.

"Hello, friend," she answered the phone.

"Hi, friend. I miss you," James said.

Charlotte started blushing and smiling.

"Look over to your right."

Charlotte looked over to her right and saw headlights flash twice. "Oh my, James, it that you?"

"Yes," he said. "I need to see you. I can't stop thinking about you; I don't know what you've done to me!"

"James, I can't leave the party. I'm sorry."

"Aw, ok. I thought we could get a quickie."

"I would love to but I can't. I've got to go; I will talk to you later."

"Ok, I will talk to you later."

When the party was over and everyone had left, Charlotte was preparing to tie up the trash and go to bed when Lloyd walked in, drunk.

"I saw you and Donte," he said.

"Lloyd, you're drunk. Please, I don't know what you're talking about."

"You want some young cock, don't you?"

"No, I don't, Lloyd. Go to bed."

"I know you want to fuck him," Lloyd accused, grabbing Charlotte's arm.

Charlotte yanked away. "Get off me!"

Lloyd slapped Charlotte so hard her lip busted. Charlotte put her hand to her face and lip; taking it away, she saw blood on her hand.

"What's wrong with you! I can't do this anymore!" she said, walking out the kitchen.

"Don't walk away from me, you whore! I know the look you gave Donte. I watched you two the whole night!"

145

Charlotte was so scared she ran upstairs to lock herself in the bedroom. Lloyd was kicking and banging on the door, drunk and raging. "Open this damn door, bitch!"

"No, Lloyd. Go away, leave me alone!"

Lloyd was so drunk he could barely stand. He continued banging on the door until he got tired; then he stumbled to his study and fell asleep. Several minutes later Charlotte went to the study to check on him. He was damn near dead. Charlotte went back downstairs to take the trash out, but when she opened the trash bin and closed it she was startled by someone saying, "Hey, you."

It was James, in the dark behind the tree.

Charlotte jumped and moved quickly to the tree, looking around to be sure no one saw them. "What are you doing here? My husband is in his study sleeping!" She was both nervous and excited.

"I wanted to see you." He was shocked, looking at her lip. "What happened!"

"Nothing, I fell."

"You didn't fall. Your husband did this to you! He doesn't love you, Charlotte, you need to leave him."

"James, it's complicated. Please go."

"Come here so I can make it better," he said.

"No, James, I will see you another time."

"I'm not leaving until you let me help you relieve some stress. Come here."

Charlotte looked around and went over to James in the dark behind the tree. I don't have much time, Charlotte said nervously. James stood behind Charlotte and put his hands down her pants. She parted her legs and he fingered her and played in her playground until she released herself all over his fingers, then he licked it off. Charlotte was so turned and her adrenaline was running high.

"James you've got to go," she said, pushing him. "Go, please."

"Ok. Will I see you later this week?"

Charlotte smiled. "Yes, but go please."

Charlotte couldn't get Donte or James off her mind after that night. She thought, *What is wrong with me?*

*****

Things were getting complicated for James. He realized that he was in love with both Lloyd and Charlotte. His plan had backfired; he was only supposed to use Charlotte to get her to leave Lloyd, so he and Lloyd could be together. Now that he had fallen in love with her, he had no idea what to do.

*****

Charlotte was in a stupor since finding out that Donte and Liz had gotten engaged and that they had set a date to get married the next summer. Charlotte didn't hear it from Donte, she heard it from Lloyd, while they were getting ready for bed.

"We're invited to the wedding," he said.

"What wedding?" she asked, as if she didn't know.

"Donte and Liz. I told you last week, they are getting married."

"Oh yeah, sorry. I forgot," she said.

"Good. I have some work to do—I'll be in my study."

"Ok," she said. "I'm going to watch the news and go to bed."

Lloyd walked out the room. Charlotte couldn't wait for Lloyd to shut the study door so she could call Donte.

"Hello?"

"Hi, Donte."

"Hello, Mrs. Web."

"Cut the "Mrs. Web" BS, Donte. I heard the news. It would have been better coming from you."

"I know, and I'm sorry. I love Liz and I asked her to marry me."

Charlotte's voice got even quieter. "Ok, well that means we're over for good."

"You told me it was over a long time ago."

"Yes," she said, "but you didn't listen! That didn't stop you before. Now you're getting married. What about us?"

"What about us, Charlotte? We both know you're never leaving Lloyd, and I'm not going to continue being your dirty little secret." Charlotte heard Liz call Donte's name in the background. "I have to go," he said.

"Donte," Charlotte said, "you will always be tangled in my web."

Donte immediately hung up.

CHAPTER FIFTEEN

After several weeks of Tabatha trying to get in touch with Roger to give him a heads up about the visit from his wife, Roger finally answered the phone. Tabatha sounded scared and anxious in a way he'd never heard her sound.

"It's important—we need to talk," she said as soon as he picked up.

"What now? What's wrong with you?"

"You would want to stop by soon. I really need to talk to you tonight."

"Look, I will see, but I can't promise anything."

"Roger, it's about your wife!" she said.

"My wife! What about my wife?"

"Look, Roger, she's crazy! Stop by tonight, please!"

"Ok, ok, calm down," he said. "I will be there."

*****

Diane and Roger had a dinner date planned for that evening. Roger called to tell Diane he had a meeting and had to cancel their plans. She had been looking forward to her date with her husband and was disappointed.

Diane made it her business to drive by Tabatha's job and house several times during the week, but tonight was different. Roger had said he needed to go downtown to a meeting and not to wait for him for dinner, but something in her gut told her he was lying. Diane got in the car and drove to Tabatha's building. She sat in the car across the street and called Roger.

"Hello, Di."

"Hi baby, what are you doing?"

"I'm on my way to my meeting."

"Ok," she said. "I was just calling to say hi. I miss you and was thinking about you."

"Baby, I miss you too! I love you, beautiful."

"I know. See you tonight."

Roger hung up the phone feeling awful. He hated lying to Diane, but he had no other choice, if he wanted to keep Tabatha away from Diane

Diane sat for several more minutes, but with no sign of Tabatha she decided to head home. She put the car in drive to pull off and couldn't believe her eyes at what she was seeing. Her heart dropped out her chest—it was Roger, pulling into the parking lot of Tabatha's building.

Out loud, she said to herself, "What the fuck? Is he messing with this bitch?!" Angry and not sure of what to do, Diane decided to wait. After twenty minutes, Diane went to the door.

When Roger had arrived at Tabatha's door twenty minutes earlier, she had opened it immediately.

"I've been trying to call you for weeks! Your wife came to my job."

"What!" Roger exclaimed, nervously pacing the floor. "When?!"

"A few weeks ago. She popped up out of nowhere. I was so scared by the way she looked at me."

"When was this again? Roger asked

A few weeks ago? Tabatha said loudly

What did she say? She didn't mention anything to me!"

"She threatened me. She said if I didn't stay away from you and her house that she would deal with me."

Roger was holding his head in panic. "Fuck, fuck, fuck, I have to go!"

When Roger immediately opened the door to leave, Diane was standing in the doorway.

Diane pushed past him through the door. "Really, Roger!!! Where is that bitch!!"

Roger tried to hold Diane back and calm her down. "Di, wait, it's not what you think!"

"Not what I think, Roger! Not what I think! How long? How long has this shit been going on?!"

"Wait, Di—"

"How long!" she demanded, her eyes tearing up.

"Di, let's go home."

"No, Roger. Move. Get the hell out my way. Since you don't want to answer me, let me ask this bitch." Diane looked at Tabatha with fury. "How long has this been going on?!"

"Look, I'm not a bitch—" Tabatha started saying, only to be interrupted by Roger.

"Di, nothing is going on! I love you. Let me explain!"

"Explain what, Roger? You can't explain what I see!"

"Tell her, Tabatha, that there's nothing between us!"

"Really, Roger," Tabatha said. "We were in a relationship for a whole year."

"Baby," he turned back to Diane, pleading and begging. "It was nothing! Please, let's go home. Let me explain."

"Get off me!" She yanked away from Roger. "Don't touch me, and I'm not going anywhere until I get the truth."

Roger hadn't seen Diane this angry in years. "I'm sorry, Di."

Tabatha took it upon herself to explain. "Diane, I met Roger two years ago. You were on your book tour. Roger came into the club with his buddies, several times a week. This one particular day he was drunk, I never seen him that drunk before, going on and on about the two of you not being able to have children. He was hurt..."

"Tabatha, don't—" Roger said.

"Shut up, Roger!" Diane yelled, heartbroken.

"Then tell her the truth, Roger!" Tabatha yelled, started to cry.

Roger was at a loss for words, seeing the tears rolling down Diane's face.

"So you two were in a relationship for a year," Diane said. "How often did the two of you meet?"

"Once a week, when you would go out of town," Tabatha answered.

Diane looked at Roger with disgust. She walked over to him and slapped him as hard as she could. "How could you, Roger? She knows so much about us and you're telling me it was nothing? Look at me!"

"Di, please, I'm sorry. I was here to break it off! She came back threatening me. I didn't see her for two year and then she popped up saying that I used her, and she was going to blackmail me, saying she was going to tell you. I couldn't let

154

that happen. Please baby, I don't want her," Roger pleaded, moving toward Diane.

Diane pulled away from Roger. "Get away from me, Roger. Don't touch me! I have one last question," she said to Tabatha. "Have you been with my husband since you've been back?"

Roger cut in. "No, we haven't, Di, I swear!"

"I've had enough, Roger," Tabatha yelled. "You used me! Tell the truth—the night of the grand opening he didn't have a meeting. He came over here and I gave him "good head", that's what he said. That was our first time since my return."

"So you gave my husband "good head", she said, walking toward the door.

Roger looked at Tabatha, then back at Diane. In a rage, Diane ran over to Tabatha and punched her in the face. Tabatha fell to the floor and Diane was kicking her. Roger jumped up to pull Diane off Tabatha.

Diane was crying, fighting off Roger trying to hold her back. "Get your hands off me! Don't you ever touch me again! Come get your things out of our house!"

"Di, please, baby don't do this, please." He was on his knees, begging. "Please, baby, I'm sorry."

Tabatha was crying . Listen to this shit, Really Roger, you are so pathetic. Look at you! As she screamed

Diane straightened herself up and walked out the door. Roger followed behind. They rode the elevator in silence. Diane exited and went to her car. Roger didn't say a word because he knew it would get ugly. When they got home, Diane slammed the door in Roger's face.

"Please, Di. Let me talk, please."

Diane was walking around the house crying, furious and hurt.

"Talk about what? We have nothing to talk about. You had Tabatha to talk too, obviously. I've been nothing but true to you! You told me you understood when we couldn't have a baby. It would have been fine if it was one time! But a year, Roger? A year!! You had to like her! Do you love this bitch? A damn whore! I'm not enough!" Confused, she was crying and laughing at the same time.

"No, I don't love her! Di, baby, you are all I need!"

"I've heard that before! That trashy whore wrote those hurtful things on our house, flattened our tires; she made those evil calls. Our life was a living hell, and you're telling me this wasn't a relationship!"

"It wasn't! I promise you, I told her I was married and I wasn't ever going to leave you and she got mad. Yes, I got caught up when you were gone—I made a big mistake. But I went over there tonight because I haven't been answering her and she said she had something important to tell me about you. Di, baby, please!"

"I remember that night of the grand opening and that bizarre meeting. I knew something wasn't right. I called you all night and you didn't answer. When you got home you told me you were tired and you're never too tired to fuck. The night you were coming home to discuss something with me, earlier that day when I was washing your clothes, I found the crumbled up parking ticket in your pocket, and you forgot to throw it in the trash."

"Di, how long have you known?"

"I've known for a few weeks. So I hired a private investigator who gave me all her information: where she lived, where she worked. I went by there once or twice a week but I never saw you. Did you know she's been arrested before for stalking and vandalism? You're not the first man she's done this to!"

"Baby, that's because she's crazy! She kept threatening me and finally I told her she could tell you, I didn't care anymore, I was tired of being blackmailed, and somehow, she changed up. It was nothing to me. She got angry because I wouldn't leave you. She said I used her!"

"I can't look at you right now."

Diane walked out the room, hurt and confused. Her whole world was turned upside down. She went downstairs to make some tea. She had never felt the way she felt at that moment. She didn't know what to think. Color was playing in her mind. *Tabatha is white, Roger is white, and I'm black,* she thought. She walked back into the room where Roger was just sitting there, his head in his hands.

With tears flowing down her face, she asked him, "Is it because she's white?"

Roger was shocked and hurt that she would think that. He jumped up to go to her. "Oh, Di, honey, you know color has nothing to do with anything. I've loved you from the first time I met you; I didn't see any color."

Diane was looking in Roger's eyes, crying.

Roger grabbed Diane close. "Please, baby, don't cry. You know I don't like to see you cry. What have I done?"

Diane pulled herself away from Roger. "Don't touch me! Get your things out of our room and move your things to the guest room!"

"Di, please baby, don't do this. Come here."

"No, that night of the grand opening, I remember very clearly, you came home and fell asleep. You were tired," she said, shaking her head, "from having your dick in her mouth. The same dick I suck and fuck!"

Roger had never see Diane get to this point. She had gotten mad before, but not like this.

Roger got down on his knees again, begging. "Baby, please, what can I do to fix this?"

"You shared your feelings with that bitch! She knew the most intimate thing to me that hurt me! When I couldn't have your child, did you truly know how hurt I was, not being able to have a baby with the man I love and want to spend the rest of my life with?" She was sobbing.

"Di, I was wrong and I'm sorry. Baby, please forgive me."

"Please move your things to guest room."

"Di, really?"

"Really," she said. "Or else I will leave." She turned to leave the room.

Roger jumped up. "No, no! I will move my things to the guest room."

"Right now," she said, dead serious.

Roger went to their room and moved his things to the guest room.

CHAPTER SIXTEEN

A few months passed, and it was as if Diane and Roger were roommates. She hadn't cooked. Although she kept it cordial as they passed one another in the house, they hadn't had sex, and she didn't talk much, only small talk.

It was early in the morning when Diane got a call from her publicist. "Hey, Diane. I have good news!"

"Give it to me," Diane said. "I need to hear some good news."

"Now that the book is complete, we have a book signing planned this weekend in DC."

"Wow, really? That's great news. How long will I be in DC?"

"A week. We leave Friday, and we have you booked at the Hilton in downtown Northwest."

Diane smiled for the first time in months. "Ok, got it!"

*****

Diane was thinking about her situation with Roger. They hadn't had sex, although he'd been trying. She wanted to, but it didn't feel right. She missed her husband but she needed time to heal. Every time she looked at him, she thought about Tabatha and the things he did with her, those thoughts made her nauseous.

Her thoughts were interrupted by the sound of Roger's keys. He came in and went straight to his office. Diane waited a little while, debating whether she wanted to tell him about her trip. She finally decided that she should; he deserved that much.

Diane knocked on the door of his office.

"Come in," he said, looking up at her eagerly.

"Hey," she said.

"Hey, how are you? You look nice."

"Thank you," she said, stiffly. "As you know, I finished the book. I have a book signing planned this weekend. I'm leaving Friday to go to DC for a week."

"Great, Di. We can celebrate when you get back."

"Oook," she said. "I'm going up to start packing, and I will see you when I get back." She turned to leave.

Diane was shocked that he hadn't asked to go, but after everything that was going on, she was sure he just didn't know what to say or do at this point, so he didn't say anything. He'd been giving her space and trying to make small talk. She knew he loved her—she didn't doubt that—but to know he reached out to another woman for comfort while she was away, going through the painful thought of not being able to have his child, really hurt her deeply.

"Di, wait. Congratulations."

Diane paused, a slight smile pulling the corners of her mouth. "Thank you. That means a lot. Well, if you need me, I'll be staying at the Hilton in downtown Northwest." She walked toward the door again.

"Di," he called out to her.

"Yes?"

"I love you."

"I know," she said, and she walked out.

*****

Diane been gone for a few days. She and Roger spoke on and off, but not like before when they had known each other's every move. It wasn't like them to not talk. Roger decided to call Diane's cell but there was no answer. He called the hotel room, and there was no answer there either. He knew she was busy but she'd never been too busy to talk to him. Something

162

didn't seem right, so Roger canceled all his meetings for the next couple of days and booked a flight to DC.

*****

Lloyd was having lunch at the café when James walked up.

"Hey man," James said.

"Hey," Lloyd replied, looking around. "How did you find me?"

"I figured you would be here. We need to talk about us and where our relationship is going."

Lloyd looked puzzled. "Relationship?"

"Yes, relationship. You can pretend all you want, but I will not be your "boy toy" anymore. We are getting too old for that."

"We've talked about this. No matter what I will never come out as gay. I'm not gay, and my family and position have no room for that. What I do is my business."

"That doesn't work for me anymore. If we can't have a relationship, then we can't have anything at all."

"James, you will continue to be my boy toy and things will stay the way they are. You are my best-kept secret."

"That's the problem," James said, angrily. "I don't want to be your best-kept secret! I want more time with you. If you can give me more time, we will see where this will go."

"Ok, James, calm down," Lloyd said, looking around again to make sure no one was noticing. "Can we talk later? I will stop by later."

Without a word, James got up and walked out the door.

*****

Diane was exhausted after four days of interviews, photo shoots, and book signings. She decided to draw a nice bubble bath. She put her hair in a bun, slid her beautiful brown frame into the tub, laid her head back, closed her eyes. But all she could think about was Roger and how much she loved him. She felt like her whole world had caved in. The tears started flowing as she thought about how she missed her friend. But then her mind reverted to those other thoughts: he had confided in another woman at a time in their lives that was difficult for them both. It made her question who Roger was— yet she still missed him so much.

Diane reached for her phone to call him, but there was no answer. Diane started allowing her mind to wander; maybe he was with Tabatha or someone else. She stopped that line of thought, thinking, *I can't allow my mind to do this. I have never questioned my marriage or his love and loyalty, now it's all on the line.* Diane got out the tub, drying off, and there was a knock at the door. She wrapped her towel around her.

"Yes, who is it?"

"Room service."

Diane opened the door slightly. "I'm sorry, I didn't order anything."

"These are for you." Diane opened the door and the concierge rolled in a cart with several dozens of colorful roses, a bottle of wine on ice, and a candlelight dinner.

"Ma'am, I'm sorry, but I didn't order any of this." Diane had her back turned to the door, smelling the flowers. "Thank you ma'am," Diane said to the room service woman. "

When she turned back around, Roger came through the door.

"No, baby, I ordered it all for you," he said.

When Diane heard Roger's voice, her heart started beating fast and tears falling. She had so many mixed emotions, but she ran over and jumped in Roger's arms. Her towel fell off; she was holding Roger so tight.

Roger had his face in her neck, holding her tight. "Damn, Di, I've missed you. I've missed holding and touching you."

Diane put her finger over Roger's mouth. "Shhh...make love to me."

Roger had thought he would never hear those words again. He was caressing her body with his fingertips, slowly and gently, sucking and nibbling on her breast, kissing every tear away.

"I love you so much, Di. I've missed you. I'm nothing without you—my days, weeks, and months have been empty. I can't live without you," Roger said, tearing up. "I'm sorry. I'm so, sorry." He burst out crying.

"I know," Diane said, through her own tears. "I missed my friend; I love you so damn much."

"I've been taking my time. I've been waiting, wanting, and praying that I could get my Di back. I want you to trust me again. I made a mistake, and I'm sorry, Di."

Diane wiped Roger's tears away. She had never seen Roger cry; he had shared a part of himself with her that told Diane he was truly sorry.

"Open wide, baby, I want to taste you."

Diane spread her legs so wide, and Roger gave her head like never before. Her tears were flowing; it felt so good. She could feel his love and his remorse. Roger didn't want Di to move; he wanted to make love to her missionary style with her legs spread wide, so he could look in her eyes as he made love to her heart, mind, body and soul. He went so deep inside Diane's good-good, it was so intense that it blew Diane's mind. Roger came so hard and strong inside her, Diane could feel it.

Roger and Diane spent the next few days shopping, eating, sexing, clubbing, and having a good time before returning home. On the way home, Diane got a phone call from the police letting her know that Tabatha had been caught lurking around their house and was arrested.

*****

Charlotte couldn't get Donte and the fact he'd broken off their relationship because he was getting married in a few weeks off her mind, so she texted him.

"Hey, are you busy? I wanted to talk."

"Hey," he texted back. "No, I'm not busy, but that wouldn't be a good idea."

"Oh, really," she wrote back, annoyed.

"I think it's best we stay away from one another," he said.

"Why?" she asked, disappointed. "You want me to do that thing with my mouth one last time? I know she's not giving it to you like I do, and what she don't know won't hurt her."

Donte was at a loss for words. He missed Charlotte, but Liz was a good woman with morals. But Charlotte was an older woman who knew what she was doing and he wanted it so bad. "Give me a few minutes to get away," he told her. "I will call you in thirty minutes."

Charlotte was excited. "Ok, see you soon!"

Before she knew it, Donte was tapping on the back door. She grabbed him, quickly undoing his belt buckle at the door, and pushed Donte back against the wall.

"Wait, Charlotte, we shouldn't be doing this."

"Yes we should—relax."

Charlotte put Donte's erect penis in her mouth and slowly and gently sucked and slurped.

"Damn," Donte said, grabbing Charlotte's head. "Oh shit, I missed this, your mouth is like a vice grip." With head laid back, eyes closed, Donte couldn't help himself. "Damn, I'm getting ready to cum!" He pulled Charlotte's hair back holding her chin, as he slowly guided her mouth over his penis.

With her mouth full of cock, Charlotte said, "Cum in my mouth."

"Damn, I'm cumming," he said, grunting loud and hard, he left his load in her mouth

Donte buckled up his pants as Charlotte stood up, looking mischievous.

"Why are you looking at me like that?"

"You're getting married," she smirked.

"Yes, I am."

"You know, we can continue to see each other."

"How?"

"Very easily, now that you're part of the Web Family, Lloyd and Liz are always working or out of town. Remember, that's how you and I met, with Lloyd being gone all the time."

"I don't know. Mr. Web gave me a chance, and this is how I repay him."

Charlotte walked over to Donte, took a hold of his face and gently kissed him. In a serious tone, she said, "Donte, let me worry about Mr. Web. You belong to me, Liz can marry you, but you will continue to be my best-kept secret."

"Charlotte, what are you talking about?" With a puzzled expression, he said, "Look, I have to go."

"Donte, it's over when I say it's over. You're caught in my web," she said, straightening his shirt.

Donte never knew that Charlotte was this devious. She took off her clothes and stood butt naked in the doorway. "Donte, come here," she said, motioning with her finger. She started rubbing and groping Donte's penis through his pants.

"Charlotte, stop. It's getting late, and I have to go."

"Just five minutes—I feel you swelling."

Donte looked at Charlotte's ass and immediately got a hard on.

"Mmhmm, I knew you couldn't resist me," she said, feeling his penis get harder and harder in her hand.

Donte grabbed Charlotte. "Come here—turn around."

Donte bent Charlotte over the couch and pounded her doggy style. He couldn't control himself. He tried, but Charlotte was Donte's addiction.

"You know I can't hold out! Oh shit, I'm cumming!"

"Cum, Donte."

"I'm cumming," he exclaimed, pounding harder and deeper. "Damn, Charlotte, this shit is so good!!! Awwwwww!"

Charlotte stood up and walked toward the door. "Now you go home to your little girl, and we will continue to see each other—or else you won't have a job."

Donte was at a loss for words again. He hadn't known what he was getting himself into with Charlotte. He knew this wasn't right, but he also couldn't stop seeing her. He was tangled in Charlotte's web.

*****

Lloyd and James had been spending a lot of time together, hanging out and chilling at James's place. James hadn't spoken to Charlotte since showing up at her house the night of the promotion party.

One day, Charlotte decided to ride over to James's house to surprise him since he hadn't been answering his phone. When Charlotte arrived at James's building, someone was coming out the door, so she didn't have to buzz him to let her in the building.

When she knocked on James's door there was no answer. She decided to go check the parking garage to see if James's car was there. In the parking garage, she saw James's car and, parked next to it, a truck that looked like Lloyd's. As Charlotte got closer she could see a guy's head laid back on the headrest and another head going up and down. As she got even closer she couldn't believe her eyes: it was Lloyd and James, and James had Lloyd's cock in his mouth!

"Oh my God," she screamed, tears leaping to her eyes. Shocked, she covered her mouth in total disgust. "No!!!" She fell into another car, stumbled, and almost lost her balance running to her car.

Lloyd opened his eyes shocked, it was Charlotte. He immediately pushed James off him. "Oh shit, what the hell is she doing here?!" he yelled, banging his hand on the steering wheel. He jumped out of the truck to run after Charlotte.

Charlotte was running and crying, unable to breathe. "Noooo!!!!!!" she yelled as Lloyd chased her.

"Charlotte, please let me explain!" he called after her, a mixture of nervousness, fear, and embarrassment running through him.

"You stay the hell away from me!" she screamed, hysterical and crying.

"It's not what you think!"

Charlotte made it to her car, got in, and locked the doors. She couldn't see a thing through the tears.

Lloyd got to Charlotte's car and started banging on the window. "Wait, please, Charlotte!"

Charlotte backed her car out so fast she almost ran over Lloyd. "Get the hell away from me, you disgust me!"

"Charlotte, please calm down—it's not what you think!"

Charlotte drove off and Lloyd ran to his truck, jumped in, and followed Charlotte home. She was speeding and swerving all over the road. Lloyd was concerned—how could he be so careless? When Charlotte got home, she hit the curve in the driveway, went up on the lawn, and left her car parked there. She ran to the front door, but she dropped the keys trying to open it, and Lloyd caught up to her.

"Wait, please, calm down!"

"Get your dirty hands off me," she said, looking at Lloyd with disgust. "Don't touch me or come near me." She was crying so hard she was coughing. "You make me sick!"

"Charlotte, please don't say that. Let me explain!"

"Explain what, Lloyd? That you're gay?!"

"I'm not gay!"

Charlotte was laughing and crying at the same time. "Really? Then what the hell was that? Now I'm dumb. You never loved me—you used me. You're gay! You were getting your dick sucked by a man!"

"I'm not gay; I'm bisexual."

"Bisexual! Really, Lloyd? Bisexual! Oh, this is funny," she said, still crying and laughing.

When she was finally able to get in the house, Charlotte went into her closet to grab a bag and started throwing things in it. Lloyd walked over and started taking things out.

"Please, Charlotte, you're not going anywhere. This has nothing to do with you—it's me. Charlotte, please don't go. You're the only one who understands me! I'm sorry, please let's talk."

Charlotte sniffled, trying to talk through her angry tears. "Ok Lloyd, let's talk. Now I know who and what has been

173

keeping you away on those late nights and when you go out of town on business trips. Please explain before I go!"

"Charlotte, I can't let you go, baby. You're my wife and I love you."

Charlotte slapped Lloyd hard and started beating him in his chest, crying and screaming, "You don't love me!" She looked at Lloyd as if she had said something wrong. "Explain, Lloyd!"

"It started in college. I found myself being attracted to both men and woman. I really never pursued any men until I met James. We had the same problem: we both dated woman, we both couldn't tell our families, and you know my career won't allow it."

Charlotte's eyes were swollen from crying. "Why did you marry me? To cover it up?!"

"No, because I love you, Charlotte. I stopped seeing James, but we started seeing each other again five years ago after I ran into him at a conference in DC. One thing led to another and I saw him on occasion."

Charlotte was in a daze, gazing out the window, feeling confused and deceived. She turned around to face Lloyd. "I have one question: do you love him?"

"Charlotte, don't, please."

Charlotte started getting loud and angry again, walking closer to Lloyd. Lloyd had his face in his hands.

"Answer me! Do you love him?!"

Lloyd looked up at Charlotte with hurt and pain. "No, I don't," he said, softly.

Charlotte was gesturing with her hands to say that she didn't understand and needed more explanation.

"One more thing: do you do him or does he do you?"

Lloyd didn't want to have to explain this. Angrily he said, "I don't get banged in my ass and I don't suck dick! I do him and he sucks my dick—are you happy?!"

"What about me!" she asked, crying and pointing to herself. "I'm going to get an HIV test tomorrow! I can't even look at you. I'm leaving and I'm not coming back. You two can have each other—I hate you!"

"Charlotte, you're not leaving." Lloyd was getting angry as he walked toward Charlotte. "Please, you're not going anywhere. You are my wife and we will work it out. I can change, and I will break it off." He begged, "Please, don't go."

"Get away from me! Work what out? I want a divorce!"

Lloyd's heads almost exploded when Charlotte said the words he didn't want to hear. "Charlotte, you belong to me!" he said, hitting his chest and getting louder and louder. "If I can't have you, no one will!"

"Do as you please!" Stuffing more clothes in a bag, she screamed, "You want the truth?" Turning around to look at Lloyd, she pointed out, "You never asked how I happened to walk in on you." She laughed and walked right up to Lloyd so they were standing eye to eye. "Well, let me tell you: I was seeing James too. We've been having long nights of sex and he's been eating my kitty kat.

Lloyd couldn't digest what he was hearing. Did he just hear Charlotte say she's been having an affair with James?

"You've been what?! What the hell are you talking about?"

Charlotte was losing her mind. "Yeah, you weren't the only one fucking James! I've been fucking James for six months now. I was going over to bang his brains out, but he was sucking your dick." She laughed hysterically.

Lloyd couldn't believe James would do that to him. He was furious that James was fucking his wife!

Lloyd turned away from Charlotte, walked out the door, got in his truck, and headed back over to James's place. He was speeding, thinking about what he was going to do when James opened the door. Lloyd left the truck in the middle of the street; he jumped out without turning the engine off and he took the stairs two at a time. Lloyd was banging on James's door, and James came running and yanked the door open.

"What?!" he yelled

As soon as James opened the door, Lloyd punched him in the face. James fell back and Lloyd continued to pound him with punches.

"You common bitch! You've been fucking my wife!" Lloyd yelled, looking James in the eye while holding him tight around his collar.

James laughed with blood trickling off his lip. "My plan worked! Yes, I was fucking her, and it was good. I was hoping we could all be together." He was laughing but could hardly move.

"Go to hell, man!" Lloyd yelled as he threw James to the floor. "Don't come near me or wife ever again, you hear me? Or I will kill you!"

James lay on the flooring, laughing as Lloyd stormed out the door and headed home. When Lloyd pulled up to the house he didn't see Charlotte's car. He ran in the house to see that her closet and drawers were empty. All of her things were gone and she had left a note.

"Dear Lloyd, please don't come looking for me. I need time to think. You're not who I thought you were, and I'm not who you think I am."

Lloyd dropped down on his knees with the letter and started crying. He knew that was the end…

EPILOGUE

So much had changed within the last two years.

Roger and Diane finally had a handsome baby boy named RJ. Diane had gotten pregnant the night Roger showed up at the Hilton in DC for Diane's book signing.

Lloyd and Charlotte both stopped seeing James and went to therapy. Unfortunately, they divorced but remain friends.

Charlotte and Donte broke it off.

Donte and Liz got married and had twins. Donte got a promotion and moved to DC to be the director of the Finance department.

Tabatha was arrested and had a warrant from another state, where she is currently on probation.

The End

AFTERWORD

We never know what life is going to bring: the right, the wrong, the ups, and the downs. We have to remember that what we do to others will come back to us, whether it's good or bad. Always remember: karma has bad timing. What's done in the dark will surely come to light and you will definitely reap what you sow. It's part of life; it's the universal law.

I thank you for your support.

ABOUT THE AUTHOR

Tina "Tee Tyme" Mitchell is an author and creator of Urban Erotica residing in Hagerstown, MD. Born November 30, 1972 in Olney, MD, she has been married for 23 years. She's a mother of three and a grandmother of four. Her writing was a hobby until she was inspired by her husband and older sister to publish her work.

Writing is her passion. She has a natural ability to write and communicate with her woman's "sexual voice" of freedom, desire, pleasure, and passion. She's in touch with her sensuality and sexuality. She's comfortable exploring your deepest sexual desires.

9 781794 676077